THE
GHOST WORE
YELLOW SOCKS

JOSH LANYON

mlrpress

MLR Press Authors

Featuring a roll call of some of the best writers of gay erotica and mysteries today!

Maura Anderson	Storm Grant
Victor J. Banis	Wayne Gunn
Laura Baumbach	J. L. Langley
Sarah Black	Josh Lanyon
Ally Blue	William Maltese
J. P. Bowie	Gary Martine
James Buchanan	Jet Mykles
Dick D	Luisa Prieto
Jason Edding	Jardonn Smith
Angela Fiddler	Richard Stevenson
Kimberly Gardner	Claire Thompson

Check out titles, both available and forthcoming, at
www.mlrpress.com

THE GHOST WORE YELLOW SOCKS

JOSH LANYON

mlrpress

Copyright 2008 by Josh Lanyon

Published by
MLR Press, LLC
3052 Gaines Waterport Rd.
Albion, NY 14411

Visit ManLoveRomance Press, LLC on the Internet:
www.mlrpress.com

Cover Art by Deana C. Jamroz
Editing by Judi David
Printed in the United States of America.

ISBN# 978-1-934531-14-3

First Edition
2008

CHAPTER ONE

There was a strange man in Perry's bathtub. He was wearing a sports coat — a rather ugly sports coat. And he was dead.

Perry, who had just spent the most painful and humiliating twenty-four hours of his life, and had driven over an hour from the airport in blinding rain to reach the relative peace and privacy of the chilly rooms he rented at the old Alston Estate, stood gaping.

His headache vanished. He forgot about being exhausted and starving and soaked to the skin. He forgot about wishing he was dead, because here was someone dead, and it wasn't pretty.

His fingers still rested on the light switch. He turned the overhead lights off. In the darkness, he heard rain rattling against the window; he heard his breathing, which sounded fast and scared; and from the living room he heard the soft chime of the clock he had bought at the thrift store on Bethlehem Road. Nine slow, silvery chimes. Nine o'clock.

Perry switched the light back on.

The dead man was still in his bathtub.

"It's not possible," Perry whispered.

Apparently this didn't convince the corpse, who continued to stare at him under half-closed eyelids.

The dead man was a stranger; Perry was pretty sure of that. It — he — was middle-aged and he needed a shave. His face was sort of greenish-red, the cheeks sunken in as though his features were slipping. His legs stuck out over the side of the tub like a mannequin's. One shoe had a hole in the sole. His socks were yellow. Goldenrod, actually. They matched the ugly checked jacket.

The stranger was definitely dead. His chest wasn't moving at all; his mouth was ajar, but no sounds came out. Perry didn't have to touch him to know for sure he was dead, and besides that, nothing on earth would have made him touch the corpse.

He couldn't see any signs of violence. There didn't seem to be any blood. Nor water. The tub was dry and empty — except for the dead man. It didn't look like he had been strangled. Maybe he had died of natural causes?

Maybe he'd had a heart attack?

But what was he doing having a heart attack in Perry's locked apartment?

Perry's glance lit on the mirror over the sink, and he started, not immediately recognizing the pale-faced, hollow-eyed reflection as his own. His brown eyes were huge and black in his frightened face; his blond hair seemed to be standing on end.

Backing out of the bathroom, Perry closed the door. He stood there trying to work it out through the fog of weariness and bewilderment. Then, eyes still pinned on the closed door, he took another step backward and fell over his suitcase, which was still sitting in the center of the front room floor.

The fall jarred Perry's thoughts into some kind of order — or at least action. Scrambling up, he bolted for the apartment door. His fingers scrabbled to undo the deadbolt.

He yanked open the door, but it banged shut as though wrenched away by a ghostly hand, and he realized the chain was still on. Fingers shaking, he unfastened that too and slammed out of the apartment.

It seemed impossible that the hall should look just as it had when he had trudged upstairs five minutes earlier. Wall sconces cast creepy shadows down the mile of faded crimson carpet leading to the winding staircase.

The long lace draperies stirred in the window draughts. Nothing else moved. The hall was empty, yet the disturbing feeling of being watched persisted.

Perry listened to the sound of rain whispering against the windows, as though the house were complaining about the damp, the wood rot, the mustiness that permeated its aged bones. But it was the ominous silence on the other side of his own door that seemed to flood out everything else.

What was he waiting for? What did he expect to hear?

Despite his desperation to get downstairs to lights and people, he felt peculiarly apprehensive about making the first move, about making a sound, about doing anything to attract attention — the attention of something that might wait unseen in the dim recesses of the long hall.

He had to force himself to take the first step. Then he barreled down the hallway, narrowly missing the half-dead aspidistras in their tall marble planters. Despite the reassurances of his rational mind, he kept expecting an attack to launch itself from the cobwebbed corners.

Reaching the head of the stairs, he hung tightly to the banister to catch his breath. His knees were jelly. Uneasily, he looked behind himself. Nothing but the twitching draperies stirred the gloom. Perry headed down the stairs. Fifteen steps to the next level; he took them two at a time.

Reaching the second floor, he hesitated. Ex-cop Rudy Stein lived on this floor. An ex-cop ought to know what to do, right?

Mr. Watson had also lived on this floor, but Watson had died a week ago in Burlington. His rooms were locked, his belongings collecting dust waiting for a man who would never return.

Not that Perry believed in ghosts — exactly — or was too chicken to face another dark, drafty hallway, but after that moment's hesitation, he continued down the rest of the grand staircase until, at last, he reached the ground floor which served as the lobby of Mrs. MacQueen's boarding house.

Someone was just coming in the front door, pushing it closed against the sheets of rain. Overhead, the chandelier tinkled musically in the gust of the storm's breath, throwing eerie colored red shadows across the man's figure.

He wore a hooded olive parka, and for a moment, Perry didn't recognize him. In fact, he couldn't see any face at all in the cowl of the parka, and (his nerves shot to hell) he gasped, the soft sound carrying in the quiet hall.

Shoving the hood back, the man stared at Perry. Now Perry recognized him. He was new to Mrs. MacQueen's rooming house, an ex-marine or something. Tall, dark, and hostile.

Perry opened his mouth to inform the newcomer about the dead man upstairs, but the words wouldn't come. Maybe he was in shock. He felt kind of funny, detached, rather light-headed. He hoped he wasn't going to pass out. That would be too humiliating.

"What's with you?" the man said. He was frowning, but then he was always frowning, so there wasn't anything in that. He actually wasn't *that* tall — a little above medium height — but he was muscular, solid. A human Rock of Gibraltar.

Finally Perry's vocal cords worked, but the man couldn't seem to make out his choked words. He took a step closer. His eyes were blue, marine blue, which seemed appropriate, Perry thought, still on that distant plane.

"What's the problem, kid?" the man asked brusquely. Obviously there was a problem.

Breathlessly Perry tried to explain it. He pointed upward, his hand shaking, and he tried to get some words out between the gasps.

And now the corpse upstairs was the second problem, because the first problem was he couldn't breathe.

"Jesus Christ!" said the ex-marine, watching his struggle.

Perry lowered himself to the carpeted bottom step of the grand staircase and fished around for his inhaler.

§ § § § §

Perfect ending to a perfect day, Nick Reno thought, watching the queer kid from across the hall sucking on an inhaler.

The divorce papers had arrived that afternoon, but what should have felt like relief felt like another failure. The job at the construction company hadn't panned out, either. It was the wrong time of year for construction — the wrong time of year for everything, it seemed. And now this. For the last few hours Nick had been hanging on to the idea of a stiff drink and some solitude, and what he got was this damn boy having hysterics.

"Kid, pull yourself together." What was his name? Something Foster. Nick had noticed it on the mailbox in the lobby.

The kid continued to huff and puff, his thin chest rising and falling with the struggle to breathe. Maybe he'd just missed an episode of his favorite soap opera. Maybe they had discontinued his favorite flavor at Starbucks. Who the hell knew? Queers.

Nick looked around the suspiciously silent lobby. Where were all the busybodies who normally littered the halls of Mrs. MacQueen's nuthouse?

"I could use some help here," he called out, whether to the Almighty or the closed doors, he wasn't sure. But after a moment he heard a chain slide. Deadbolts began scraping, latches cranking, turn knobs clicking. Old Miss Dembecki's door opened a crack.

The kid, who had turned a lovely shade of blue, lowered the inhaler long enough to wheeze, "There's a…dead man —" Suction resumed.

"There's a *what*?" Nick demanded. "Where?"

People were now creeping out of their rooms into the hall. Miss Dembecki, wired for sound in pink curlers, pulled a gingham nylon bathrobe around her skinny body. "What's happened?" she demanded querulously. "What did you do to him?"

"I didn't touch him." Nick glanced up as a floorboard creaked.

Suspended above them was a white moon of a face. Stein, the ex-cop, shone down on them. His mouth made an O as round as the rest of his perspiring face: round eyes, round mouth, squashed nose. "What's going on? Somebody in an accident?" His voice floated down.

Dourly, Nick eyed the kid. "I don't know."

"Perry, whatever's wrong?" quavered the old lady.

Perry. That figured, Nick thought grimly. A pansy name if there ever was one.

Across the hallway another door opened.

A cat wafted out of the Bridger woman's apartment and pussyfooted toward them, white plume tail waving gently. The kid made a panicked sound and pointed with his free hand.

Nick pivoted impatiently, but Ms. Bridger, six-feet-nothing, red haired, and clad in an emerald kimono, was already scooping up the offending feline and shutting it back in the apartment.

Dembecki called, "Miss Bridger, perhaps you... Something's happened to Perry." She cast an accusing look in Nick's direction.

Nick began, "Look, lady —" then gave it up, stepping aside as Jane Bridger rustled up in her silk dressing gown. There was a dragon embroidered on the back of her gown. She was doused in Poison perfume. Nick recognized it as Marie's favorite, and his stomach knotted.

"Perry, sweetie," she cooed, joining the kid on the bottom step. "What's wrong?" To Nick she explained, "He has asthma."

"I noticed."

Foster lowered the inhaler once more and got out, "Dead man...in my...bathtub."

He was speaking to Nick as though somehow it was Nick's problem; maybe he thought Nick was the only one equipped to deal with a dead body scenario.

The door to the landlady's apartment opened at last, and Mrs. MacQueen billowed out in a cloud of cigarette smoke. "What's all the racket?" she rasped. "What are you people doing now?" A blast of canned TV laughter followed from her rooms.

"Perry's ill," Miss Dembecki quaked. "It's his asthma."

Bridger patted Foster's shoulder kindly. Her long fingernails were blood red against his white shirt. "Hang in there, sweetie. Take slow, deep breaths." Her robe slipped open to reveal the outline of breasts so perfect they had to be fake. Nick raised his eyes. If Stein leaned any further over the banister he was going to take a nosedive.

Two small dogs burst out of MacQueen's rooms, and nails slipping on the hardwood floor, scrabbled their way to Bridger's door, barking hysterically.

Fed up, Nick stepped back, treading on Miss Dembecki's slippered foot; he hadn't noticed her sidling up behind them. Now she yowled like an injured cat.

"Sorry," Nick exclaimed.

"Why can't you look where you're going?" moaned Miss Dembecki, hobbling to one of the overstuffed chairs by the fireplace. The fireplace was unlit. It had never been lit as far as Nick could tell. Maybe it was supposed to be decor. It just emphasized how unwelcoming the damn house was.

Foster gulped out more vehemently, "There's a dead man in my bathtub!"

Dead silence. Another burst of televised laughter. Someone tittered nervously.

"What does *that* mean?" demanded MacQueen finally. She reminded Nick of James Cagney in drag, sort of sounded like him too.

"It means somebody ought to go upstairs and check it out," Nick said.

The boy shot him a grateful look.

"Who, *me*?" MacQueen actually backed up in one of those you-won't-take-me-alive-copper moves.

"You own the place. You're the manager, aren't you?"

"But, that's...I mean...sure, but..." Her bug eyes traveled from face to face. She licked her colorless lips. The others were making sounds, wordless excuses, apologetic noises.

"Forget it," Nick said. "I'll go." It would be a relief to escape the freak show for a minute or two. "Where are your keys, kid?"

Foster said, "I didn't...lock the...door." He still sounded breathy, but he wasn't blue anymore. He kept a tight grip on the inhaler.

"It's the third floor. The tower room opposite yours," informed Nick.

"Got it." Nick started up the stairs.

On the second floor, he passed Stein, who twitched him a meaningless smile but didn't speak.

Nick continued his climb to the third floor. It was dark and quiet up here; the scent of cats and the sound of TV didn't reach. Neither, half the time, did the heat. Lace curtains over the poorly sealed windows floated up like specters, then flattened back against the wall. Not the best visibility: the long hallway was badly lit; a pair of half-dead plants on tall pedestals provided suitable cover for ambush.

A funny feeling prickled across the back of Nick's scalp. It was a feeling he had learned not to ignore during fourteen years in the service — though unexpected in a broken-down mansion in the middle of the Vermont woods.

He considered, and discarded, going back to his quarters and arming. He was pretty confident he could handle any garden-variety scumball who might have sneaked in.

Approaching the kid's apartment cautiously, Nick turned the doorknob.

The door swung open onto a large chilly room that smelled of rain and turpentine. It looked more like an art studio than someone's living quarters. The curtains had been removed to allow more light. A spattered drop cloth covered much of the floor. A canvas half-covered with inky pine trees rested on an easel near the window. Blank canvases were stacked against the wall; painting utensils covered what appeared to be the dining room table. There were paintings everywhere: on the walls, on the floor.

In the middle of the room was a suitcase.

So the kid had been gone overnight; that meant someone could conceivably have got into his rooms and…dropped dead.

Except the bathroom door was open, the light on. Nick had a clear view of the tub. It was empty.

Surprise.

Had he really expected to find a dead man in a bathtub?

Nah, but something had sure scared the shit out of little Perry. The few times Nick had passed him on the stairs he seemed quiet, polite, and reasonably sane.

Nick advanced down the hallway.

The bathroom was big, old-fashioned, the twin of his own. The tub was one of those claw-foot porcelain jobs, running hot and cold water through separate spouts, making it ideal for scalding your feet. There was a small, bullet-shaped window over the tub. For laughs Nick opened it, gazing down on distant muddy ground and tree tops sparkling wet in the house lights.

Nobody and no body.

There was a streak of brown on the inside of the tub. He knelt to check it out. Red clay? Paint? Rust? That smear could be a lot of things, and yet instinctively the hair rose on the nape of his neck. He scratched at it with his thumbnail, sniffed his thumb. Was he imagining that coppery, metallic smell?

No damn way.

He noticed black scuff marks on the tile. Like somebody's heels were dragged across the floor?

Nick's eyes narrowed thoughtfully. Rising, he made for the bedroom. Not much to see. A twin-size bed, a battered bureau. The only thing out of order was one brown shoe lying in front of the closet. He picked it up. Cheap leather. Size 14. There was a hole in the sole. Nick set the shoe on the window ledge, glancing at the bed. A stack of books sat on the night table. Library books. *I Like 'Em Tough, They Can't All Be Guilty, I Found Him Dead, Secrets of a Private Eye.* A bookshelf was packed with paperbacks flaunting equally lurid titles.

His mouth curved wryly. Okay, now things made sense.

Still, remembering the terror in those wide brown eyes, he opened the closet door. Oh boy. The kid even hung up his pajamas.

He glanced under the bed. Someone had raised their little boy right. No dust bunnies, no dead bodies.

Cursorily, Nick glanced through the other rooms and closets. No corpses. There was an asthma chart pinned to the refrigerator, which told its own sad little story, and a box of Froot Loops on top of the fridge, which Nick found grimly amusing.

As he shut the front door, the painted canvases lining the living room caught his attention. Nick didn't know anything about art, but he knew what he liked. He liked these. There was a sureness and maturity to these calm studies of covered bridges and autumn woods that one wouldn't expect. Chalk one up for the boy next door.

The landing on the second floor was deserted when Nick reached it. Stein had either got bored or fallen over the balcony. Same scenario in the front lobby. MacQueen had escaped back inside her apartment and turned up the TV volume. In fact, the only people left were Foster, who seemed to have recovered somewhat — the inhaler was no longer in sight — and the voluptuous Ms. Bridger, who stood before the unlit fireplace.

"All clear?" she inquired cheerfully. Her red hair and green dressing gown were like a shout in that drab room.

"Yeah." Nick remembered the streak of red clay on the tub and dismissed it.

"No way. That can't be!" Foster's thin face tightened. "Then they moved him," he said stubbornly.

"*They?* What, it's a conspiracy?"

Foster flushed. He had that baby-clear skin that advertised his emotions like a billboard.

"Sweetie, sweetie," cooed Bridger. "Couldn't it have been a bad dream?"

"Or too many detective stories?" Nick put in.

Foster was still sitting on the bottom step or the grand staircase. He glared up at Nick. "I wasn't asleep!" He turned that angry gaze toward the Bridger chick. "I got back from the airport, walked in, and there he was. I wasn't sleeping. I wasn't hallucinating."

"There's no dead body now."

Foster swallowed hard. "I think we should call the police."

Bridger looked in dismay to Nick. How was it Nick's problem? Let them call the police. Just leave him out of it.

"But, sweetie, Mr....uh. Mr. —"

"Reno," Nick supplied reluctantly.

"Mr. Reno has already checked. The police won't find anything now. Right? We don't want to cause trouble."

Nick glanced at her. Maybe a little hard around the edges, but still a surprisingly good-looking woman to be living out here in the middle of nowhere. What was it about the cops that worried her?

"The police have forensic people," Foster said stubbornly. "Trained people who have equipment that can find microscopic traces of blood or hair."

Nick thought of the bloody streak in the tub again. The possible scuff marks on the tile. "Listen, kid —"

"Perry. Perry Foster." Foster rose as though he had made up his mind.

"Whatever. Foster, the police are not going to send out their forensics team in the worst storm of the decade because of a crank call."

"I'm not a crank! There was a dead body. Someone put him in my *locked* apartment and took him away again. Someone in this house."

Bridger glanced nervously at MacQueen's closed door. She chewed her bottom lip and said, "Sweetie, let's the three of us go inside my apartment and think this through."

Nick opened his mouth, but Foster beat him to it. "I can't go in there," he said obstinately.

"I'll put the cats away."

"Their dander —"

"Oh, for cryin' out loud!" Nick exclaimed. "I don't care what you people do, just don't involve me."

The kid, Foster, gritted his jaw, but his eyes were glittering ominously as he stared at Nick. "Sure. Thanks for your help," he managed, politely.

Nick started to turn away. "The police might want to question you, Mr. Reno," Bridger warned. Her eyes glittered like green glass.

Nick drew a deep breath and exhaled slowly. "Let's go inside and talk this over," he said very calmly.

§ § § §

The police arrived while they were having coffee. The coffee was laced with brandy, which was a mistake in Nick's opinion, but clearly the whole night was a mistake as far as he was concerned. Calling the cops was the biggest mistake, and he had waxed loud and eloquently — but mostly just loud — on the topic.

Now he was brooding in silence, taking up half of Jane's horsehair sofa. The police, having heard Perry out, tramped upstairs to investigate. Nick Reno had been right. There was no forensics team, just two weary and wet deputy sheriffs in yellow slickers, looking mighty unamused.

Before the deputies headed upstairs, Nick filled them in about the mud smear on the tub and the scuff marks on the tile.

"How come you didn't mention those things before?" Perry accused when the door closed on the officers of the law. "Those are clues."

"Let the cops decide if they're clues or not," Nick returned.

"More brandy?" offered Jane. He held out his cup, and she topped off his coffee.

Perry stared down at his mug. He knew the other two were irritated with him for insisting on phoning the police; it was like they were operating in an alternate universe. Of course he had called the police. Any normal person would call the police.

So now the three of them sat waiting for the law to finish, drinking spiked coffee and eating decorated cookies hard enough to crack a tooth on. The brandy was getting to Jane; she was flirting with Nick.

Perry's gaze wandered around the room. There were two Christmas cards on a table. One was from an insurance company. The other was lying face down. Jane was not the Suzy Homemaker type. Her apartment was a mess. She must dress and undress walking from room to room, he decided, eyeing a silk blouse draped over a lamp shade. The tabletops were dusty, and there was cat hair on the overstuffed furniture. His chest tightened as he noticed it.

"How are you feeling now, sweetie?" Jane asked Perry, as though reading his expression.

"Fine." He shot a diffident look at Reno and then looked away. Nick Reno was staring at him like he was a dork.

"What happened while I was upstairs?" Reno questioned suddenly.

Jane shrugged and pulled at the shoulder of her slipping dressing gown. "Nothing."

"Mr. Center came out of his rooms," Perry offered.

"For about half a minute. He went straight back inside," Jane clarified. "Everyone did. Miss Dembecki went back in her apartment and locked the door. Ditto Mrs. Mac. It's not like anyone thought you would find anything." She patted Perry's hand apologetically, asking Nick, "Why? What did you expect?"

Nick Reno had the kind of face that gave nothing away. Instead of answering Jane directly, he asked, "How many people live here?"

"Seven, now that poor Mr. Watson is gone."

Nick's eyes narrowed reflectively. "That's the guy who died in the village? And Stein is the fatso on the second floor?"

"That's right. He works as a security guard at the mall most nights. It used to be Mr. Stein, Mr. Center, and Mr. Watson on the second floor. On this floor, it's been me, Miss Dembecki, Mrs. Mac, and Mr. Teagle since…well, it feels like forever. I'm sure you've met Mr. Teagle. He makes a point of meeting everyone." Her smile was sardonic. Mr. Teagle did not approve of Jane. "And way up on the third floor, it's just you and Perry in your twin towers."

Perry was trying to work out a timetable. There was no way anyone could have entered the house from the outside, or if already inside, use the main staircase without coming into view of the tenants crowded in the lobby. That meant that whoever had moved the body must have still been on the third floor during the time between Perry's flight and Nick's trip upstairs. Maybe the intruder had been in Perry's rooms when Perry found the body. Maybe he had been watching from behind the door the whole time.

It was an unsettling idea. "The body must be hidden somewhere on the third floor," Perry told them.

Jane quit tapping her carmine nails on her cup and stared.

"Where? My rooms?" Reno suggested dryly.

Perry's eyes narrowed, focusing on the notion. That *was* the most obvious explanation: there was no body because Reno had carted it off to his own rooms. He had been outside when Perry came downstairs. Could that mean anything?

Watching him add it up, Reno commented, "You've got a hell of an imagination, kid." And strangely enough, Perry was reassured.

"Maybe it went down the laundry chute. The corpse, I mean." Jane handed round the plate of wreath-shaped cement cookies.

Nick declined cookies with a shake of his head. "Describe this dead man to me," he ordered.

Perry thought hard. "He was about fifty, heavy-set. He needed a shave. His hair was reddish, like he dyed it. He was wearing a yellow and brown checked sports coat and mustard-colored socks. He had a hole in his left shoe."

Nick went on alert. "What kind of shoe?"

"A brown loafer."

"You're sure there was a hole in the left sole?"

Perry nodded, then gripped by sudden memory said, "He had bushy hair in his nostrils and a mole on his chin."

"More than I needed to know," Jane murmured.

A heavy hand pounded on the front door and she jumped. Perry faded to the color of one of the corpses in his tough guy novels. "It's the police," he got out.

"No kidding. We called them, remember?" Since the other two seemed paralyzed, Nick rose and opened the door to the deputies.

Tired and grim, the two officers of the law regarded them.

"I feel I gotta ask. Were you folks drinking this evening?" questioned the senior partner. In his rain slicker and hat, he strongly resembled the Gorton Fisherman — after hauling up an empty net.

"We had a little snort for medicinal purposes," Jane volunteered over Perry's indignant protest. "We weren't together all evening, so I can't say beyond that." She stretched comfortably, and the deputies' gazes trained on her gaping neckline.

The Gorton Fisherman harrumphed. "There's nobody upstairs. No body."

"I told you that much," Nick said. "What about the blood?"

"Who says it was blood? Could have been...mud."

"You seen a lot of blood?" the second deputy sheriff queried. He was younger and seemed a little more pugnacious about being dragged out on a wild-goose chase.

"Enough."

Perry said, "What about the scuff marks?"

"Scuff marks don't mean diddly," said the deputy. "And I didn't see any mud." He glanced at his partner. "Did you see any mud?"

"Nope. That tub was clean as a whistle. Like someone just scrubbed it down."

"What does that tell you?" Jane put in.

The older man eyed her calmly. "That someone just scrubbed it down." His dark eyes rested for a moment on the brandy bottle in the midst of the coffee table clutter.

Perry insisted, "There was a dead man in my bathtub. He didn't get there by accident."

"Maybe he wasn't dead," the sheriff said. "Maybe he was a vagrant, and he left after you found him."

There were so many holes in that theory, Perry didn't know where to start. He protested, "My apartment was locked. How could he have got in?"

"How would a dead man get in? A vagrant would have a better chance of breaking in than a dead man."

Inescapable logic. Still Perry persisted. "But he *was* dead. Someone brought him in and took him away again so you wouldn't believe me."

"It didn't take *that*," the deputy said. The older officer gave him a reproving look.

"Listen," Reno said. "I didn't believe in that dead body myself, but I saw a streak of something in that tub that sure as hell appeared to be blood to me. And there were black marks, probably scuff marks, on the floor tiles. Also, Foster said the dead man was wearing a shoe with a hole in the sole. I found that shoe. I left it on the windowsill."

"We didn't see any shoe with a hole in it."

"Did you check the bedroom?"

"Sure. We weren't looking for footwear specifically."

"Did you see the shoe on the windowsill?"

The deputies exchanged doubtful looks.

"I didn't see any shoe," said the Gorton Fisherman. "You want to check for yourself," he added, "be my guest."

"I'll take your word for it," Jane said. She smothered a yawn and said to no one in particular, "Gentlemen, I hate to be a party pooper, but I need my beauty sleep." She made a lazy shooing motion, and the minions of the law obediently retreated further into the hall.

"You're damn right I'll see for myself," Perry said, rising. But he couldn't help checking to see if Nick was along for the ride.

Nick was on board all right. He marched up the stairs, kid and cops trailing, and let himself into the Foster boy's apartment for the second time that evening.

Perry followed him in, staring around the rooms like he'd never seen them before. The night was taking on a hallucinatory quality. Granted, he was somewhat sleep deprived. He stared at his suitcase in the middle of the floor. It seemed a lifetime ago that he had walked out of Marcel's wood-framed Victorian and caught the plane back to Vermont.

He trailed Nick into the bathroom. Sure enough, the tub was empty — and sparkling clean.

Nick ran his fingers along the rim. "Damp," he commented. Perry stared at him. The deputies crowding the doorway also stared at him.

Pushing through them Nick headed toward the bedroom, zeroing in on the windowsill.

A shoe stood in plain sight on the ledge. It was black, small — maybe a size 9 — in good shape.

A muscle clenched in Nick's jaw as he examined the loafer. "This isn't the shoe."

"See for yourself, buddy. It's the only shoe here."

Nick tossed the shoe to Perry, who caught it and swallowed. "This is my shoe," he said as though he feared his shoe was guilty of some misdemeanor.

"Yep, that's what we figured."

"I thought you didn't notice any shoes?" Reno retorted.

"We didn't notice any *suspicious* shoes."

"Shut up, Abe," the older deputy muttered.

Nick started to speak, then bit it back. This was a losing proposition. The cops had made up their minds about twenty minutes earlier; that was plain.

He glanced at the kid, and it was obvious that Foster knew it was all over, although he was gazing at Nick expectantly. Why? What did he imagine Nick could do about this? Even if Nick wanted to do something about it.

He stared back, and the kid looked away, gritting his jaw. His hands were shaking and he shoved them into his pockets.

The deputies took their leave.

"We'll say good night, folks. Keep safe." The senior officer, last out the door, tipped the brim of his rain-spattered hat.

Nick caught the door before it closed on their heels. He glanced back at Perry Foster. The kid was focused on the tub framed in the bathroom doorway.

The underbreath comments of the deputies died away with the sound of their boots on the staircase.

Situation defused, Nick thought. Rack time at last. "I guess that's it," he said. "I guess I'll say good night too."

Foster's head jerked his way. "You're going?"

"Yeah." Nick was elaborately casual in response to the note he didn't want to hear in Foster's voice. "It's all clear here."

Foster was a frail-looking kid. He lived on his own and presumably held a job, so he couldn't be fourteen, though that's how old he looked. His wrists were thin, and bony knees poked out of the holes of his fashionably ripped Levi's. There were blue veins beneath the pale skin of his hands. Nick thought of the Froot Loops cereal and the asthma chart on the refrigerator.

Hell.

"Thanks," Foster managed huskily. "I know you probably think I'm psycho too, so I appreciate your helping me."

"I don't think you're psycho." Actually he had no idea if the kid was psycho or not. "I think you saw something. But whatever it was, it's gone now. It's over."

Nick thought of the shoe with the hole in it; he should have noticed right away it was too big for a pup the size of Foster. Someone had switched that shoe after Nick left. Someone had swabbed down the tub and the floor. Someone had balls of steel. But it was not Nick's problem. It was not his job to save the world. Not anymore.

"Yeah, well…" The kid managed one unconvincing smile. "Maybe I can get a hotel room in town." He picked up his suitcase. "I don't want to stay here tonight."

Nick's nod was curt. Great idea. Best idea yet. Except… A gust of wind shook the house. The lights flickered. From across the room, Reno heard Foster give a soft gasp. His eyes looked enormous. Like Bambi after his mom bought it in the woods.

It was a dark and lousy night. Not a night to be out driving if you didn't have to. The radio crackled with weather advisories. Anyway, what kind of bastard would send an asthmatic kid out in a rainstorm?

"Hell," he growled. "You can stay with me tonight."

There was that wash of color in the pointed face. "I don't want to be any trouble," Foster said hopefully.

Nick snorted.

CHAPTER TWO

"You were a marine?" Perry tried to make polite conversation while sizing up Nick Reno's apartment.

The tower apartments were small and secluded and mirrored each other. In both, the main room stepped up into a round dining alcove with two diamond-paned windows. From outside, the rounded rooms looked like small towers. They gave the rambling old house a vaguely gothic look. Otherwise, the place was unremarkable, especially now that most of the internal architecture had been gutted to accommodate apartments. Nick's place had a long, narrow kitchen facing the woods. Perry's overlooked the overgrown and mostly dead garden. It didn't matter because his rooms were just a place to paint. It didn't look like Nick spent a lot more time in his. He had two bedrooms (the one Perry could see into had been turned into a weight room) and a bathroom. There was little furniture and few personal effects.

Reno slid the deadbolt home and answered shortly, "Navy SEAL."

"Let the journey begin."

Nick gave him that hard look that Perry was beginning to recognize, and Perry explained, "On the TV commercials. *Let the journey begin.* Like, *It's not just a job, it's an adventure.* The marines slogan, you know."

Apparently Nick did not know. He disappeared into the kitchen.

Feeling rebuffed, Perry turned back to the front room. The walls were bare except for one painting, a giant seascape. It hung over the fireplace. Gray-blue waves beneath lowering skies. Perry liked it. There were no other pictures. None. The walls were institutional white. There was a short blue couch, where he'd be spending the night. A standing light was positioned over the sofa. A small coffee table stood before it.

That was it for the furniture. None of it revealed anything of Reno's personality unless absence of furniture revealed something.

"You want a beer?"

Perry set down his suitcase and followed Nick's voice to the kitchen. The kitchen was immaculate. An old-fashioned fridge hummed senilely to itself. The gas range looked like an antique. The clock on the wall indicated that it was after midnight, and Perry realized just how tired he was.

Nick stood at the sink chugging down a beer. Coming up for air, he said, "Help yourself."

Perry opened his mouth to decline, but he saw the glint in Nick's eyes, the look that said he expected Perry to be a finicky little candy-ass who didn't drink beer at midnight.

"Thanks," he said and opened the fridge. He expected it to be empty of anything but alcoholic beverages and health supplements. Wrong. The metal racks were stuffed with food. Milk, eggs, bread, and meat wrapped in white butcher's paper. Vegetables pressed up against the crisper pans like damp noses.

Perry found a beer — good imported ale — and tried to twist off the top.

Nick inhaled his own beer and spit it out coughing over the sink. He was laughing, not very kindly. Perry rubbed his hand on his jeans.

"You need a bottle opener," Nick informed him, wiping his chin with the back of his hand.

Defensively, Perry muttered, "I wasn't paying attention."

Nick passed the bottle opener. "How old are you? You're over twenty-one, right?"

"I'm twenty-three."

The dark eyebrows rose skeptically. Nick looked about thirty. He had smooth olive skin and short, dark hair. And those navy blue eyes. He was very good-looking in a stern *no trespassing* way. About the same height as Perry, but built for action. Key word: muscles.

Perry swallowed a mouthful of beer, the faint skunky taste marking it an import.

He couldn't decide if he *liked* Nick Reno, but he felt safe with him. He couldn't imagine anything happening that Nick Reno couldn't handle.

Nick left the kitchen and disappeared down the hall. Perry drank some more beer.

Pinpricks of rain against the ink black windows had a mournful sound. He remembered that just a few hours ago he had been in San Francisco. He couldn't handle that memory now. Not with dead men appearing and disappearing like the middle reel of a slasher movie. He swallowed another musky mouthful of beer.

"How long have you lived here?" Nick's voice inquired from the other room.

"A year next month."

"And nothing like this has ever happened before?"

"No, of course not."

"Anything suspicious?"

Perry thought it over. "No."

"You don't sound convinced." Nick appeared in the doorway with a couple of folded wool blankets.

"It's an old house," Perry said reluctantly. "It's got...atmosphere."

Nick's expression indicated he hoped "atmosphere" wasn't catching. "What, floorboards creaking? Whispering voices?"

"Sometimes I feel like I'm being watched," Perry said. "Sometimes it seems like my stuff has been moved. Like somebody's been in my rooms. Sometimes it seems like the house is...listening."

Nick considered him for a long moment. "I'd say you were nutty as a fruitcake, except someone scrubbed down that tub and switched those shoes. I sure as hell didn't imagine it. And I sure as hell can't think of any innocent reason someone would do something like that."

It was a huge relief to be believed. Perry volunteered, "I was supposed to be gone all this week. I came back early."

"Who knew that?"

Perry rubbed his eyes with the heel of his hand. "I don't know. It wasn't a secret. Janie — Ms. Bridger — knew. Mrs. Mac." It was all beginning to catch up with him. Swallowing hard against the tightness in his throat, he said, "I'd been planning the trip to San Francisco for weeks. I guess anyone could have known."

Whatever Nick read in his face caused him to say brusquely, "Yeah, well, it would be helpful to narrow it down. Get some sleep, and we'll talk in the morning."

Sleep sounded like a good idea. Perry hadn't eaten anything in almost twenty-four hours, and the beer was hitting him hard. Or maybe it was exhaustion. He hadn't closed his eyes last night — and the night before that he had been too keyed up to sleep. The drive from the airport had taken everything he had; he had been sputtering along on empty for hours now.

"Thanks." He dropped down on the sofa. Nick tossed him the folded blankets. He caught them against his chest.

He opened his mouth to thank Nick one more time, but Nick, had already disappeared down the hallway to the room Perry couldn't see. The door closed with finality.

The closed door was a relief. Perry hadn't realized how nervous the older man made him. Nervous and self-conscious. Nick Reno, man of action, clearly despised the wuss from across the hall.

Perry opened his suitcase, found flannel pajamas and a clean pair of socks. It was going to be a cold night. Nick's thermostat was set on sixty, and the window casements leaked.

Hands shaking with sudden exhaustion, Perry changed into the pajamas, pulled on the socks, and rolled himself in the blankets. The couch was about a foot too short. It didn't matter; a bed of nails would be preferable to sleeping in his own silent rooms.

He vaguely considered brushing his teeth but somehow just couldn't convince himself to make the effort. Instead, he buried his face in the cool pillowcase and got a shock. The pillow smelled of Nick Reno. It smelled masculine: long-ago aftershave and some kind of herbal soap.

In some indefinable way it reminded him of Marcel, although Marcel had smelled nothing like Nick Reno. Perry's sense of loneliness and loss returned in force, crashing over him like a wave, dragging him out to sea on an emotional riptide. His eyes prickled, his face flushed. He pressed closer to the pillow that smelled like Nick Reno to muffle the sob that threatened to tear out of his throat.

Truly the last fucking straw if he finished this weekend crying himself to sleep on Nick Reno's sofa. He pictured Reno coming out to find him sobbing into the upholstery and surprised himself with a watery chuckle. He could imagine the horror on Reno's face so clearly.

Listening to the rain thundering down, he closed his eyes and let it wash him away.

§ § § §

Thirty minutes, Nick thought, slapping the magazine into the MK23. Thirty minutes tops and the kid would be in dreamland.

He waited, stretched out on the bed, arms folded behind his head, at ease, waiting.

He liked the sound of the rain battering down against the walls and roof; it reminded him of the sea. He missed the sea.

When the clock clicked over the thirtieth minute, he rose soundlessly and went to the door to ease it open.

All quiet in the living room. The light was still on, though, so he waited, listening. He focused hard, tuning out the rain, tuning out the clock, the branches scraping the house. He could hear the kid breathing softly, evenly, asleep.

Opening the door wide, he stole down the hallway. His houseguest was curled up uncomfortably on the sofa. His suitcase was open, his inhaler was propped on the coffee table in grabbing reach. His keys were on the floor. Nick took a second look. Foster wore some kind of striped PJs and a wristwatch.

Nick picked up the keys, pausing when a floorboard creaked. The kid sighed and buried his face deeper in the pillow.

Nick continued toward the door. Unlocking it, he slipped out into the dim hall. He relocked the door.

Cautiously he made his way down the hall. There was a walk-in linen cupboard at one end. Doubtful, but he wanted to check it out.

A steamer trunk beneath one of the grimy windows caught his attention. Talk about your long shots, but Nick had learned a long time ago never to assume anything. He turned his flashlight on.

The trunk was locked, but he picked the old lock without much trouble. Lifting the lid, he was greeted by the scent of mothballs. The interior was stuffed with junk: a couple of battered photo albums, old *Life* magazines, a black doll missing an arm, draperies that looked like shrouds. He shut the trunk, snapped off his flashlight, and headed for the linen closet.

A relic of more genteel times, the walk-in closet opened with a lugubrious screech of unused hinges. Nick waited for the sounds of alarm, ready to abort.

Nothing. He pulled the chain of the overhead light bulb. Tired light flooded empty, dirty shelves and cobwebs big enough to accommodate a Jules Verne spider. Dust carpeted the floor; Nick didn't need to get down on hands and knees to verify that no one, dead or alive, had been in this room for years.

Strike two.

The kid — or maybe it had been the Bridger woman — had mentioned a laundry chute. Nick ran the flashlight beam along the wall. He had a vague memory of laundry chutes in hotels. Usually they opened out into the basement. Shoving it down a laundry chute might be a good way to get rid of a corpse, but there didn't seem to be a chute door on this floor. The two tower rooms mirrored each other, and since there was no laundry chute in Nick's room, he was pretty sure the kid didn't have one, either.

That meant someone would have to lug the corpse down to the second level and stuff the body into the laundry chute there. Most of the chutes Nick had seen weren't that big. It might be a good way to dispose of a child or a midget; an adult-sized corpse was liable to get stuck in place.

He proceeded along to the Foster boy's apartment, feeling inside the unlit rooms for the light switch.

Briefly, he was distracted by the spread of painted canvases. White church steeples against stormy skies, a lonely, windswept red barn, golden trees: New England autumn. What did Foster do with all this? Did he try to sell it? It was better than a lot of stuff Nick saw for sale.

He studied the meticulously cared-for brushes, the tantalizing tubes of color, the sponges, rulers, razors, knives, rolls of canvas. An expensive hobby, if that's what it was.

Opening the bedroom window, he stared down at the tall ladder glistening in the light coming from behind him. Here was the most likely explanation. The window had no screen, and it was large enough to push a man through.

But when Nick had checked, the window was locked. How did someone stuff a body out through a window, climb out themselves without dropping the body, close the window, and then *lock it from the inside*?

For that matter, how did an intruder get *in* through a locked window?

Okay, say the window hadn't been locked to start with. Still no easy task to cart a deadweight up a twenty-foot ladder. Going down, the killer could just drop his load, but even that was a risk. Someone might hear the body crashing against the house. It might hang up in the trees. Shoving a corpse out of a window presented a number of logistical problems.

But a man might be desperate enough to try. Mostly it would depend on the size of the body and the size of the man carrying the body.

Wind skulked around the house, rising up to rustle the wet leaves with a ghostly hand.

Nick shook his wet head like a dog and ducked back inside the apartment.

The intruder would have to be a man, he decided. A man in good shape. Nick was in great shape, but he wasn't sure he could tote a dead body too far, unless the deceased had been the size of someone like Perry Foster. And judging by the size of that missing shoe...

It had to be an inside job. Nothing else made sense. Nick contemplated the other male residents of the Alston Estate. David Center sounded like a wacko, but he was blind, which probably put him out of the running for Psycho of the Year. Rudy Stein on the second floor was a possible. Teagle on the first floor was another screwball: one of those hale and hearty old farts who had a habit of sticking his nose into other people's business.

But Teagle was away visiting relatives in Barre. It seemed unlikely that he'd drop in just to deposit a body and manage to split with no one the wiser.

Which brought him back to Stein and Center. Stein was an ex-cop according to scuttlebutt. Center was a professional psychic, a fortune-teller. He actually had a shop in Fox Run where he read palms and tarot cards. How the hell a blind man read tarot cards, Nick had no notion.

He really couldn't picture any of this crew scaling ladders in the dark of the night, with or without dead bodies. The whole thing didn't make sense. If Nick hadn't seen the scuff marks and mud-that-might-be-blood for himself, he would have pegged Perry Foster as delusional. But somebody got too clever. Switching the shoes was a mistake. It was arrogant. Practically a challenge.

Nick never refused a challenge.

§ § § § §

Perry woke after a deep and dreamless sleep.

It took him a moment to orient himself. He was not in his own bed. And he was not in Marcel's bed, either. It all came rushing back. Every morning for the past nine months his first waking thought had been of Marcel. But now, instead of the usual bloom of anticipation, a chill depression settled on him like snowfall weighing down a tree branch. He could feel his composure cracking beneath that weight; it didn't help at all to remind himself that he was grieving for a dream, for something that had never existed except in his imagination. And for someone who had never existed at all.

He wiped the corners of his eyes. It was quiet in the apartment. He listened to the drip, drip, drip of rain from the eaves. Nick Reno was already up; Perry could hear him moving quietly around the kitchen, and he could smell coffee percolating and bacon frying: two of the best aromas in the world.

His stomach growled. He fought his way out of the cocoon of blankets and dragged on his jeans. He had a crick in his neck. He needed a shower and a shave. He needed to brush his teeth.

He needed to go back to his apartment.

The realization filled him with dismay. Even in daylight the thought of going back there, of facing the silence, the emptiness — the memory of the corpse in the bathtub...

He headed for the kitchen, pulling on a T-shirt. Nick sat at the table drinking coffee and reading a newspaper. He glanced up, his eyes dark blue in his bronze face.

"Morning," he said laconically. "Help yourself to coffee."

There was an old-fashioned stainless steel coffeepot sitting on the range. Perry moved to the stove. A clean mug sat on the counter, which seemed a friendly gesture. He poured coffee: strong, plain coffee. None of that fancy, flavored java for Nick.

"There's milk in the fridge," Nick told him without looking up from the paper.

Pouring a lot of milk and a couple of spoonfuls of sugar in his coffee, Perry sat down across from Nick. He watched Nick swallow black coffee. Nick finished the story he was reading and neatly folded up his paper. Catching Perry's eye, he nodded curtly.

"Sleep okay?"

"Yes, thanks."

That seemed to cover the small talk. Nick pushed back his chair, went to the fridge, and took out a carton of eggs. He moved efficiently around the kitchen; he drained the bacon and cracked the eggs.

"Sunny-side up?"

"Huh?"

"Your eggs. Fried okay?"

"Sure," Perry said. "Thanks." He was happy all out of proportion to be invited to breakfast, to delay going back to his own rooms. "Thanks for letting me crash here last night," he said rather shyly.

Nick flipped butter over the eggs, not answering.

He wore Levi's and a blue plaid flannel shirt. The shirt was unbuttoned, hanging open to reveal a stomach as brown and hard as a ship's figurehead. His chest muscles rippled as he tilted the heavy iron pan. Perry warned himself not to stare.

Nick possessed a great profile too, maybe not typically handsome, but strong and symmetrical. There was both character and toughness in his face. Perry wanted to sketch him.

He could imagine what Reno would say to that idea.

"How long were you in the SEALs?" he inquired, breaking the silence.

"Ten years. Fourteen years in the navy altogether."

"That's a long time."

Nick shot him a wry look. "More than half your lifetime."

"Did you like it?"

"Why? Thinking of enlisting?"

The sarcasm caught Perry off guard, and he hid himself in his coffee cup.

Maybe Nick thought that was ruder than called for. He said, "What do you do with all those paintings in your apartment?"

"I try to sell them."

"To who?"

"To anyone. Why, want to buy one?"

Nick gave him a level look and then grinned. The smile was very white in his olive face and unexpectedly youthful. It transformed him, just like smiles in books were supposed to do.

"Maybe," he said. "You're not bad."

At this unexpected praise, Perry felt himself flushing. Nick seemed like someone whose idea of art would be girly calendars or plastic-framed posters of hot cars. But that wasn't fair, because there was that moody seascape hanging over his fireplace.

Perry volunteered, "A couple of gift shops carry my work. I'm trying to get one of the galleries to consider me. So far, no luck." He shrugged.

"Did you go to art school or something?"

Perry's stared down at the patterns in the grain of the tabletop. "No. I wanted to go to art school, but it…fell through."

"Yeah?" Nick didn't sound too interested. He set a plate in front of Perry heaped with fried eggs, bacon, and hash-browned potatoes. A *lot* of food.

Perry faltered, "I usually don't eat breakfast." He was pretty sure Nick would not consider the delicious offerings from Kellogg's a proper kick-off.

"Big mistake. Breakfast is the most important meal of the day." Nick said it deadpan; clearly *daily nutritional requirement* was not something he took lightly.

Perry tried the eggs. They were good. Why wouldn't they be, coated in a heart attack's worth of butter? He picked up a slice of bacon, wondering what Nick's cholesterol level must be.

Sitting down with his own plate, Nick asked, "Have you been thinking about who might have known you were supposed to be gone this week?"

Back to business. It was nice of him to take an interest, though.

"Janie, like I said. And I think I mentioned it to Mr. Teagle. And Mrs. MacQueen."

"Anyone else?"

"Here, no. I told them at the library because I was taking my vacation."

"You work at the library?" The dark eyebrows rose as though Perry had confessed to being an exotic dancer.

"I like books." Perry added defiantly, "I like people who read." There were no books in Nick's apartment, not even a cookbook. No magazines. There was the morning paper, but did that count?

Nick's mouth twitched a little as though he found Perry's defensiveness amusing. "Someone decided to use your apartment for cold storage while you were gone, that's obvious. What doesn't make sense is all this lugging a corpse around. Why not leave him where he died?"

"Well, because it would have been incriminating."

"Sure, but because of how he died or *where* he died? Could you tell how he died? Could you tell if he'd been murdered?"

Perry remembered that green-toned face, the gaping mouth, the hollowed cheeks, and sinister slits of eyes. Nausea rose in his throat. He spoke around it. "I didn't see blood, but I didn't look carefully. I didn't touch him."

"Could he have been strangled?"

Perry shook his head. "No." He'd read enough detective novels to know what that would look like.

"I guess he could have been poisoned. What did it smell like?"

Perry stared at Nick. His stomach rolled over once and then paused for station identification. "He smelled…dead."

Nick looked unimpressed. Perry tried, "Maybe he died of natural causes, but because he wasn't supposed to be in a particular place, he was moved to my rooms."

"Why not dump him in the woods or on the main highway?"

"Maybe there wasn't time? Putting him in my apartment had to be a temporary measure."

"Maybe. I guess we need to focus on who had opportunity. You could have made up the whole story, except that I did see that smear, and the scuff marks, and the shoe, and you didn't have opportunity to get rid of those before the cops showed up. The same's true of the Bridger dame. I figure she was with you the whole time I was upstairs?"

"Well, yeah," Perry answered, surprised. "And she was never out of our sight once you came back down."

"Neither MacQueen or Dembecki could lift an unconscious man. I don't think they could do it together, let alone by themselves. That leaves Stein and Center. What do you know about those two?"

"Mr. Stein used to be a cop," Perry said. "He's retired now."

"Is he married?"

"Divorced, I think. I don't know anything about Center except that he's a medium. He holds séances. He can tell fortunes by reading tarot cards."

"In other words, he's a quack."

Perry shrugged. "He did a reading for Jane once. She said it was...uncanny."

"At fifty bucks a pop, *uncanny* is the word." Nick polished off his eggs and studied Perry's plate. "Eat up, kid."

Perry shoveled in a mouthful of hash browns and confided, "I usually can't eat when I'm nervous."

Nick shook his head. "Eating right is essential."

"Did you learn that in the SEALs?"

"As a matter of fact, I did."

Perry nodded encouragingly. He recognized a fanatic when he saw one, and all fanatics liked a chance to spread the gospel. Sure enough, Nick was on his soapbox faster than you could say *glycemic index.*

"A proper diet provides the fuel to keep your engine running smoothly. It provides energy and promotes the growth and repair of tissue. And regulates your body processes."

Perry bit back a grin. This was the furthest Nick Reno had unbent so far — in fact, he was almost friendly in his enthusiasm.

"Carbs, protein, and fat are the three energy nutrients," Nick concluded. "Best energy source is carbs." He looked pointedly at Perry's mound of potatoes, and Perry shoveled in another forkful automatically.

"Could the police be involved?" he questioned thickly and then swallowed. "They could have cleaned up the tub and switched shoes."

"Why would they?"

"Why would anyone?"

"I don't see this as an outside operation," Nick said. "Someone could have used the ladder outside your window, but he would have tracked mud and rain all over the carpet. And he couldn't have locked the window after himself."

Perry weighed this, nibbling on a slice of bacon. When was the last time he'd had bacon — good bacon that wasn't all rind? A long time. Nick ate well, for sure.

"There's another possibility," Nick added. "The murderer — assuming it was murder — could have been in your place when you arrived and moved the body after you left."

Although that thought had occurred to Perry too, he didn't like it. It freaked him out: the idea of someone watching him, maybe ready to kill him too.

"Move it where?"

"Someplace on the third floor." Nick added, "Not that I could find any sign of it."

"What do you mean?" Perry put two and two together fast. "You *checked*? Last night? You went out alone?"

"I can handle myself." Nick was amused by Perry's horror.

Meaning Perry could not?

"Anyway, the situation's secured, I guess."

"Secured, sure." That was clear enough. Perry pushed his plate away. "Thanks for breakfast and everything. I guess I should get back now."

Nick gnawed his lip. "I've been thinking about that. I don't think you should stay in your apartment till you know how this bogey is getting in and out."

"I can't afford a hotel," Perry said hopelessly. "Last night I was desperate, but…" He offered a quirky, shame-faced smile. "I'm short my rent money now. I spent — I spent too much this month."

Nick's face said it all.

"Then have MacQueen give you another apartment."

"There aren't any. Except Watson's, and all his stuff is still there." Perry shivered.

Nick said grimly, "You do what you want, kid, but I'd get the locks changed on my door ASAP." After a moment he added reluctantly, "I can loan you money for that."

"Thanks," Perry muttered humbly. "Thanks for everything."

Nick shrugged this off. He was doing the breakfast dishes as Perry retrieved his suitcase and trudged off down the hall.

Unlocking the door to his apartment, he stuck his head in and stared around suspiciously.

Everything seemed quiet and normal. He might have dreamed the events of last night. It all looked like it had before he left, giddy with happiness and excitement, for San Francisco. He remembered locking his rooms with the feeling that he was shutting the door on a chapter of his life.

A wave of depression hit him.

Dropping onto the nearest chair, he put his head in his hands and tried to deal with it. He was glad he'd managed to sleep a little and eat some breakfast, because otherwise he'd be falling apart right now. The homey rattle of the fridge, the tick of the clock; these familiar sounds seemed desolate now. Usually he liked the rain, but it wasn't helping matters today.

Rising, he carried his suitcase into the bedroom, pausing by the bathroom door just to verify that it was body free.

Everything looked spick-and-span.

Depositing his suitcase on the bed, something caught his eye. Something lay on his pillow. A bird. A brown dove, dead.

Hand shaking, Perry picked it up. It felt soft in his hand, and cold. Its neck hung brokenly.

CHAPTER THREE

Nick knew what the pounding on his door meant before he peered out the peephole. He swore and opened the door.

Perry Foster stood there cradling a bird in both hands. "It's...dead," he got out.

A dead bird. Nick processed the news. Assess and respond, that was the program, and he had best respond fast because more alarming than the dead bird was the fact that the Foster kid was blue in the face and gulping for air.

Why me? he thought. *I've got my own problems.* He took the dead bird in one hand and hauled the kid inside with the other.

"Sit."

Foster collapsed on the sofa, braced his hands on his knees, and struggled to breathe. It was not pleasant to watch. Nick felt helpless, which made him angry.

"Where's your...what do you call it? Inhaler?"

Foster ignored him, gulping like a landed fish.

"*Shit!*"

The boy's eyes shot up toward Nick's face, and he realized he was probably making it worse. Did people die from asthma nowadays? He didn't know anything about it. He took a turn around the living room and paused by the couch. Awkwardly, he patted the kid between his bony shoulder blades.

"Calm down, kiddo. You're fine now."

Foster nodded. Courteous to the last breath.

The attack went on for what seemed like forever to Nick. Absently he smoothed his hand up and down Foster's back, feeling the links of spine through the soft cotton of his T-shirt — and why the hell was he running around wearing a T-shirt in this kind of weather?

"Try to breathe slowly," Nick ordered, half-remembered TV shows flitting through his mind.

Eventually Foster's breathing calmed. "It...was on my pillow," he managed at last.

Nick had forgotten the dead bird that lay on his coffee table. He stared at the small, broken body. His head pounded with anger.

He was mad about the dumb bird, he was mad about the dumb kid, and he was mad that he was being dragged into this mess.

"Think hard," he instructed. "Is there anybody who has a grudge against you?"

"*Me?*" panted Foster. "This...isn't about...me!"

"Never mind what you think it's about. Do you have any enemies?"

"Of course not!"

"Have you had any run-ins with anybody lately? Maybe something insignificant? Playing your stereo too loud or something."

Foster shook his head.

"Any arguments over parking spaces? Cut anyone off driving to work?"

Another shake.

"Revoke any library cards?"

Amazingly, Foster laughed. It was a weak laugh, but it was a real laugh.

"You cut your vacation short. Why?"

Those wide, fawn brown eyes gazed at Nick woundedly. "My friend...changed his mind."

"Your... Oh." He thought that over. "No hard feelings on his side?"

"None." One husky word full of heartbreak. It was embarrassing. But then, prosaically, Foster added, "Anyway, he lives in San Francisco."

"Okay, anyone else you're fucking?"

The Bambi look again. Nick had the urge to smash it into pieces.

"Kid, you're queer, right? Problems come with the lifestyle."

Foster whispered, "I have a problem-free lifestyle. I had one friend. That's over."

"Well, don't cry about it." His brusque tone brought the color creeping back into Foster's white face, and that was a good sign in Nick's opinion. Foster was kind of cute in a Christopher Robin way, and unwillingly, Nick was curious about the friend who had changed his mind. "No arguments with anyone at all?"

Wearily, Foster shook his head.

"Then I guess we can assume that this has to do with the dead man you found. Someone is warning you off."

"Why? The cops didn't believe me."

Nick squeezed his shoulder — he wasn't sure why — and rose. "No, and they won't believe you this time, either."

Foster nodded at the coffee table at the broken dove. "What about that?"

Nick shook his head. "Can you prove where you found this dead bird? It could have flown against the house last night and broken its neck. It happens. The cops might think you're doing this for attention. Or that you're not right in the head."

Foster looked scared and stricken.

With a gentleness that surprised him, Nick said, "Even if they believe you, what can they do? Seriously. The most they could do is charge someone — and who would they charge? — with breaking and entering. Leaving a dead bird is not even a specific threat."

Finally Foster nodded.

Nick took it as permission to get rid of the bird. When he came back to the front room, Foster said, "What should I do?"

You're an adult. Do what you want. Nick opened his mouth to say it. He had done some violent things in his time, but that would have been punching a baby in the face; instead, he said, "Let's scope out your apartment. You can pack some things."

"And go where? I can't afford to move; I told you that. Anyway, I can't break my lease."

Not exactly outlaw material, young Foster.

Nick said, "I'd say someone getting into your apartment is pretty good grounds for breaking your lease. Make MacQueen give you Watson's rooms. She can have his gear moved out, and I'll help you move your gear in."

Foster gazed up at Nick like Nick was his hero, and Nick felt an uncomfortable tightening in his gut. Foster had nice bones, clear skin, and honey-colored hair that fell in his eyes. His eyelids were blue-veined eggshell and a pulse was visible in the vulnerable hollow at the base of his throat. Nick cleared his own throat.

§ § § §

Outside Foster's apartment they found Mr. Teagle energetically banging on the door.

A big, raw-boned man, Teagle greeted them in his booming voice. "Why, there you are! I wondered where you were, son."

Despite the smile he looked tired, grayer than usual around the edges — and every one of his seventy-something years.

"Hey there, Mr. Teagle," Foster said. "When did you get home? How was your trip?"

He was a friendly tyke, no doubt about it.

Teagle's voice rose in the manner of the hard-of-hearing. "This morning. Wish I'd never gone. Waste of time. People say the economy's improving, but I can't see it," He shook his head. "These damn Democrats." He peered skeptically at Nick. "You a Democrat?"

"I'm an Independent," Nick said shortly.

Teagle appeared unconvinced. "You're that ex-marine, aren't you?"

"That's right."

Maybe Teagle had been army. He shook his head again and turned back to Foster. "Son, they said you had a terrible experience last night. Someone broke into your apartment?"

"Someone did," Foster replied lamely, apparently having trouble putting into words the whole unvarnished truth.

"These young vandals are everywhere," Mr. Teagle said. "There's no discipline, no control. It's this permissive society. Why in my day…"

He treated them to a dissertation of the good old days while Foster unlocked the door and let them inside his rooms.

Nick wished Foster would get rid of the garrulous old fool, but he was as useless at repelling social invaders as burglars.

"Did you want some tea, Mr. Teagle? Nick?"

"No," said Nick.

"I'd love a cup," Teagle lowered his girth onto one of the chairs, apparently settling in.

"Hadn't you better pack?" Nick asked Foster woodenly.

Mr. Teagle stared at Nick over the top of his horn-rims although he spoke to Perry. "Pack? Are you going somewhere, son?"

Foster gave Nick one of those uncomfortable looks. "Maybe. Till I can sort out what's happening with my apartment."

Teagle turned the horn-rims on the kid. "Does this have to do with that burglar last night?"

"Sort of. He wasn't exactly a burglar."

"But where will you go, son? You can't break your lease." He studied Nick once more, as though suspecting he was behind it all. "This your idea, young man?"

"Yep," Nick said cheerfully.

Foster made himself scarce in the kitchen, returning finally with Teagle's tea. He said deprecatingly, "I'm just going to throw some things in a bag," and moved to hightail it down the hallway.

Mr. Teagle set his mug down on the drop cloth and said heartily, "I know! What do you say to staying with me awhile, Perry? Just till you sort out this little mix-up."

Foster halted midflight. "That's...really kind of you," he said reluctantly.

"Then it's settled!"

"Foster's staying with me for the time being," Nick said curtly, amazing himself yet again. Foster shot him one of those meltingly grateful looks that irritated and gratified Nick at the same time.

"I see," Mr. Teagle said slowly after a moment, disapproval vibrating in his tone.

Nick felt himself changing color at what the old man obviously thought. Well, let him think it; it wasn't true, and anyway...Nick didn't trust him.

"Who has keys to these apartments?" he asked Teagle. "Besides MacQueen?"

"Tiny, of course. You know. The maintenance man."

Nick blinked. How the hell had they forgotten about Tiny? Not only did he live on the premises, he was big and strong enough to tote bodies up and down ladders all day long.

"Anyone else?"

"Let me think...Hmm. I think Miss Bridger may have a copy. Mrs. MacQueen relies on her to keep an eye on things when she goes away."

He glanced at Foster who was carrying his suitcase out of the bedroom. "Son, do you think I might have a word with you in private?"

"Uh, sure." Foster glanced uncertainly at Nick.

Nick said, "I'll be down the hall."

He was shaking his head as he walked back to his rooms, wondering what the hell he'd let himself in for.

§ § § § §

Mr. Teagle cleared his throat and said, "Sit down for a minute, son."

Perry sat down. He had a feeling he knew what was coming, but he didn't know how to head it off without being rude or hurting the old man's feelings. Mr. Teagle had always been kind to him, though he was kind of a pain in the butt, checking out Perry's mail and dropping by to scope out Perry's visitors — not that Perry had many visitors.

"Son, you know I don't like to pry. It's only…Fox Run is a small town, and despite what some legislators might think, Vermont is a conservative state. You've always been discreet about your friends, which is wise. Very wise."

"It's not like you think," Perry objected stiffly. "Nick's just offering me a place to stay while I figure out what to do."

"You know how these things look, Perry. People will talk, and that kind of talk could do you a lot of harm."

Perry said, "Mr. Teagle, Nick isn't even gay. He's just…being kind."

Mr. Teagle winced at the *G* word, and said kindly, "Who's going to believe that, son?"

"Well, that's their problem," Perry said finally, politely.

"Now I'm not trying to tell you what to do, although I've lived a lot longer than you, and I know just how mean and spiteful folks can be. I think you should be very careful about making any decisions right away."

"I can't stay here," Perry said flatly. "There was a dead body in my apartment."

"You're a sensitive boy," Mr. Teagle admitted. "Are you sure you're not letting your imagination run away with you?" His rheumy brown eyes studied Perry.

"I'm sure."

"Of course, it's up to you."

"It is, yeah."

Mr. Teagle mopped his suddenly sweaty face with a handkerchief. "I think mebbe I'll go lie down; this traveling takes it out of me. I'm not as young as I used to be."

He looked the color of wallpaper glue, and Perry said, "Are you all right? Do you need help getting downstairs?"

"No, no. Promise me at least you'll think about what I've said. If you need a place to stay, my door is always open."

The old man rose and lumbered out. Perry followed him into the hall, locking the door. He waited until Mr. Teagle had disappeared down the staircase before heading straight for Nick's apartment.

He knocked on the half-open door, and Nick called from inside, "It's open."

Perry walked in. "Did you mean what you said about staying here, or should I go talk to Mrs. Mac now?"

Nick's face twisted. "I figured you didn't want to be roomies with the old coot. If MacQueen won't let you take the Watson place, you can bunk here till you figure out what to do. But don't worry. MacQueen will let you move in there; she's got a legal obligation to make sure her tenants are safe."

Perry concealed his disappointment. He didn't want to stay in Watson's apartment surrounded by a dead man's belongings; he wanted to stay with Nick, who came off so hard and cold, but who was unexpectedly kind.

They walked down to the lobby, and Perry knocked on MacQueen's door. From inside came the never-ending accompaniment of TV.

They waited.

Nick pounded loudly on the door. Down the hall, Miss Dembecki's door opened a crack and then closed again hastily.

"Maybe she's not here," Nick said.

"She's always here."

At the sound of a sliding bolt, Perry stepped back hastily. A gust of cigarette smoke and stale air escaped the vacuum, followed by a little dog so fat it could hardly waddle its frantic escape. Perry coughed nervously and glanced apologetically at Nick.

"Get that mutt!" Mrs. MacQueen's voice grated from inside the cloud of cigarette smoke.

Nick bent and grabbed the dog; its overlong nails skittered on the wood floor. He slid it back into the room like he was sliding a mug down a tap rail.

Mrs. MacQueen appeared in the mist, cigarette wagging in her pudgy face. "What is it now?"

Perry explained what it was now.

Mrs. MacQueen looked from one man to the other. Her expression grew, if possible, more unpleasant.

"You can't be serious, Mr. Foster," she said. She glanced at Nick as though wondering what he had to do with this sudden insurgency. "That room is already rented out."

"You've got to be kidding," Nick said. "Your tenant is dead."

"His possessions are still there. We haven't been able to arrange matters with his…er…heirs yet."

We? Her and the dogs?

"I'm not going to mess with his stuff," Perry said. "I just want to stay someplace where no one can break in any moment. Someone's been in my apartment twice."

Mrs. MacQueen cackled, "*Twice!* Now it's twice!" She shook her head. "Sorry, sonny, you can tell Tiny you want the locks changed on your place. I'll go that far."

"I'm not sure they're coming through the door." Perry heard himself and turned pink, but he stood his ground.

Mrs. MacQueen glowered at Nick. "Did you put him up to this?"

"Look, ma'am," Nick said, "I'm not the imaginative type, and I saw enough to convince me someone is getting into Foster's rooms."

"That ain't here nor there," Mrs. MacQueen said. "The Watson apartment is a bigger place. It costs another hundred dollars a month."

Perry's heart began to pound hard, shaking his thin frame. He said, "There's such a thing as renter's rights, Mrs. MacQueen. If you can't provide adequate security, I can break my lease. Then you'll be out my rent *and* Mr. Watson's rent."

"I'll sue you," Mrs. MacQueen threatened.

"I'll sue you back. And I'll win. People have been in my rooms. Twice. At least. Mr. Reno is a witness to that. And if you do take me to court, I'll sue you for damages too."

"I've seen screwier cases than this win in court," Nick supplied dryly.

MacQueen's eyes darted from one to the other of them as she thought this over. The dogs were scratching at the bottom of the half-closed door, their tiny paws flashing in and out from under the door.

"Okay, whatever. It's your choice," Perry said, turning away.

"Now wait a minute," Mrs. MacQueen protested. "Don't be so hasty. Young folks are always so hasty. I didn't say you couldn't rent Watson's. I said it was more than your rooms, but it's paid through the end of the month, so you could stay there, and maybe these matters will clear themselves up by then."

Battle over. Perry was all riled up and nowhere to go. He felt almost let down as he stared at her.

"But if there are any problems, if the...er...heirs claim anything's missing, it'll be on *your* head, sonny."

"Great," Nick said. "That's settled. Come on, Foster."

MacQueen's door slammed shut so hard the chandelier high above them chinked like broken glass. But then like most things around there, it didn't work anyway and hadn't for years. Nick strode off toward the grand staircase.

"I can't believe it was that easy," Perry admitted to Nick's wide shoulders.

"You amaze me, sonny," Nick threw back.

They started up the stairs and he said briskly, "We'll get you settled in, and then we'll go talk to Tiny." He was feeling more cheerful. He could stow the kid in a safe environment, and then get back to his own problems, like the fact he couldn't get a damn job because he was "overqualified."

They rounded the banister on the second landing, and Nick stopped short. Perry reached out to steady himself, touching muscles that felt like rocks beneath Nick's flannel shirt.

David Center stood before them, tall and thin in a purple dressing gown. Nick didn't think highly of men who drifted around in purple dressing gowns, although in that house nothing was surprising.

"So you've seen him," Center announced.

Nick was crisp. "Seen who?"

"The ghost of Witch Hollow."

CHAPTER FOUR

"And which hollow would that be?" inquired Nick.

Center ignored this. "Contact with the supernatural can be an alarming experience if you're not prepared. The first time I —"

Nick opened his mouth, but catching his expression, Perry forestalled him by saying apologetically, "I don't think what I saw was a ghost."

In Nick's opinion, the kid seemed to spend a lot of time making excuses for other people's lunatic expectations.

"But of course it was a ghost!" exclaimed Center, turning in the direction of Perry's voice. "You don't truly believe one of the living dead appeared and disappeared in your tub?"

Speaking of one of the living dead...Center looked like the villain in a 1940s movie. Pencil thin mustache and hair black and smooth as a raven's wing. His eyes were hidden behind dark glasses. Everything about him bugged Nick — and that was just on general principles.

"When you put it like that, a ghost does make more sense," he said sardonically. Catching Foster's gaze, he realized the kid was struggling to keep a straight face.

Which was a huge relief. For a moment Nick had pictured Foster swallowing this pap the way he ate up the pulp fiction from the library.

"I suppose you are a nonbeliever," Center said to Nick's forehead.

"I believe in plenty of things," Nick said. "But spooks aren't one of them."

Center turned away from Nick, groping for Foster's hand. Nick felt Foster go rigid beside him and wondered why he put up with this kind of crap.

"Come, you must tell me what you saw," Center breathed. "Every detail. We must determine why the specter chose to manifest itself to you."

"Can it wait?" Perry asked. "Nick is helping me move my stuff."

"*Move?*" Center was horrified. "You're not leaving?"

"Only out of the tower room."

"But you can't! That would be a great error. The spirits have chosen to contact you there. You mustn't reject them. The consequences could be grave."

"No pun intended?" Nick's tone caused the color to rush into Center's pale face. "Foster, I don't have all day."

As he continued up the staircase, he noticed one of the doors down the hall, Stein's door, closing. The guy must have been listening to their conversation. Good luck to him if he could make sense of that gobbledygook.

Perry caught him up on the third landing.

"Man, that was pretty cold," he said.

"The guy's a screwball."

Silence.

"If you feel like spending the day chatting on the astral plane, be my guest. I've got things to do."

Foster had no response to that, either.

There was more silence in Nick's apartment. He went to check his phone messages, and Roscoe had actually called.

Nick dialed the number Roscoe had left. His palms felt sweaty and cold, his heart was thumping — all unfamiliar sensations.

A receptionist put him through to Roscoe without delay.

"You asshole," Roscoe greeted him. "You better not have taken a job with somebody else!"

It was all Nick could do to say calmly, "Why? What have you got?"

"Lousy pay, lousy benefits, long hours, and a bunch of assholes to work with."

"What's the downside?"

Roscoe chuckled. "Hey, listen, the job's yours if you want it. There is a catch, though."

"Shoot."

"You need to interview with the partners. It won't be a problem, I've already vouched for you. It's a formality, that's all."

"When?"

"That's the catch. Rick is leaving for South America on the eighth, and he won't be back for a month. We could wait till then, or if you're willing, we can get you booked on a flight to the West Coast this evening. We can interview tomorrow morning, do lunch and show you around the town, and you can get a flight out the following morning. Hell, you could stay a few days and hang out, catch up on old times, scope the operation."

"I'm just treading water here," Nick said. "I'll take the plane ticket."

"That's my boy," Roscoe crowed. He said to someone offline, "What did I tell you? He's in."

Roscoe gave him the details, and Nick rang off. He realized he was grinning at the receiver, and he headed for the bedroom to throw some things into a bag.

He'd clean forgotten about Foster who was sitting on the sofa, staring at the rain trickling down the window.

"Something's come up," Nick told him shortly, because — although there was no reason to — he felt guilty. "I've got a job interview in Los Angeles, and I have to catch a plane this evening."

"I sort of figured," said Foster. He grinned. He had an attractive grin, wry and sort of sweet. "Congratulations."

Nick didn't like feeling guilty. Especially when there was no reason for it. He said brusquely, "I'll help you move some things downstairs this afternoon. We can take care of the rest when I get back."

"Nah," said Foster. "I can manage with what I've got here." He nudged his holdall. "It's not like I can't get into my apartment if I need anything."

Nick didn't know what to say.

A heavy knock on the door frame saved him from having to come up with a reply. Tiny stood in the doorway, shifting from foot to foot in restless unease. He was a big man, simple, as they used to say. He had worked at the Alston Estate for the last thirty years, long before Mrs. MacQueen had bought the isolated farmhouse to turn it into a boarding house.

Nick narrowly sized up the handyman. Tiny made a hulking figure in baggy overalls over a worn red flannel shirt. His gray head was shaved close, and his left eye had a tendency to twitch. He sort of looked like Curly of the Three Stooges, only he had no visible sense of humor.

"Mrs. Mac says you want to see Mr. Watson's room."

"Yeah, we want to see the room," Nick said.

Tiny made a great scooping motion that was evidently to urge them onward. Nick followed Foster out, and they proceeded back to the second floor.

Unlocking the door to the late Mr. Watson's room and standing back so that Foster could enter, Tiny announced, "Mr. Watson is dead."

"I know," Foster said patiently. He seemed to have patience to spare; it encouraged kooks, in Nick's opinion.

Foster wandered doubtfully around the room while Nick checked the lights, the thermostat, the hot water. Everything looked like it was in working order. The room smelled stale, of cigars and dust. Hopefully the kid's asthma wouldn't kick up.

Tiny picked up a comic book and tossed it back down nervously. "He died in the village. In the bakery."

"I heard that too," Foster said.

"He bought a cherry pie, and he dropped dead. His things are still here. This is all his."

"I won't bother his things," Foster said.

There were a lot of "things." A tall wine rack in one corner. Lots of black leather furniture. An expensive home entertainment center took up an entire wall. There were framed pulp art posters on its opposite. Big-breasted women fighting off saber-toothed tigers and one-eyed Nazis. Nice work if you could get it.

Dead fish floated in an expensive aquarium.

"Oh no," Foster said, dismayed by the tiny colored bodies littering the greenish water like flower petals. "They must have starved."

Tiny came to stare at the tank with him. He sniffed and pulled out an enormous handkerchief, blowing his nose mightily. Then he scooped his big hand in the tank and ladled out the dead fish, dropping them in an ashtray. "Nobody told me about them," he told Foster.

Tiny was great with animals, always trying to bring stray cats and dogs home, returning baby birds to nests. Gentle giant stuff.

Nick checked the windows. Watson had invested in his own security measures. No one was getting in that way.

"It seems secure," Nick told Foster, who watched him with those big brown eyes.

Tiny stared at him too. "Locks don't stop ghosts," he said.

"Not you too," Nick growled. "Is everyone here nuts?"

"I've seen him," Tiny said. "I saw him. The ghost in the yellow socks."

"Where did you see him?" Foster asked with quick interest.

Tiny's eyes shifted evasively. He shrugged. "I see him sometimes."

"Was he dead when you saw him?" Nick asked, always practical.

Tiny looked confused. "He's a ghost," he explained.

Foster said with a casualness that would only deceive Simple Simon, "Tiny, I wanted to ask you something. Do you know who has keys to my apartment besides you and Mrs. Mac?"

"You do," Tiny said helpfully.

Shaking his head, Nick turned away to investigate the bedroom.

"But anyone else?" Foster persisted. "Has anyone ever asked to borrow your keys?"

Tiny looked scared. "No."

"Are you sure?"

His eyes shifted uneasily back and forth.

"Who borrowed your keys?" Foster pressed.

More recalibrating of the eyes. Tiny licked his mouth and began to hum.

"It's okay, you can tell me," Foster said. He smiled encouragingly. "I won't tell."

"No one," Tiny said, and shrugged his big shoulders.

Nick watched this mild-mannered interrogation with increasing exasperation. It was obvious the big man was lying. He knew his own instinct to shove the guy against a wall was not a good one, but he felt pressured leaving town with this still unresolved.

"I lost them," Tiny announced suddenly. "Mrs. MacQueen yelled at me."

"You *lost* them?"

Tiny's left eye started twitching in response to Nick's tone.

"When did you lose them?" Foster persisted.

Tiny shrugged. "I don't remember. "A while back."

"Yesterday? The day before yesterday?" Nick couldn't conceal his impatience with the pair of them.

Tiny shook his head. "Mrs. Mac found them again."

"*When?*"

Tiny looked at Nick like he was the moron. "I don't remember," he said slowly and clearly.

§ § § §

"Do you need a ride to the airport?" Foster asked after Nick insisted on helping him carry a couple of boxes of his belongings downstairs.

"Nah." Nick set Foster's keys where he couldn't miss them on top of the dining room table. "I'm flying out of Burlington International. I'll leave my truck at the airport."

Foster nodded. He looked a little forlorn, more so because he was trying hard to keep a stiff upper lip.

Nick hesitated. "You'll be fine, kid. When I get back..." He didn't finish it because really his responsibility was finished here. He did not want to develop this acquaintanceship; the kid was not his type. In more ways than one.

Foster said quickly, "Oh, I'm set now. Thanks for all your help."

"One thing for damn sure, MacQueen needs to change the locks on all these rooms. Those missing keys mean anybody could get into these rooms anytime."

"Maybe Tiny just misplaced them," Foster offered hopefully.

Nick shook his head. People could be so naive. "It's kind of a coincidence, don't you think?" He considered it and said abruptly, "Let's go talk to MacQueen now."

"I don't think I should press my luck," Foster said. "It kind of undermines my argument for taking Watson's rooms if they're not any more secure than my own."

The unexpected logic of this surprised Nick. He said, "Well, I'm going to talk to her. I don't like the idea of someone waltzing into my place while I'm gone."

He started downstairs and found Foster with him. "I thought you weren't going to press your luck?"

Foster grinned that funny little grin. "I'm lending moral support."

"Is that what it is?"

"Sure."

A tinny voice drifted up to them.

"U.S. District Judge Frank Facey found Mickey 'The Chop' Cimbelli, alleged head of the Martinelli crime family, competent to stand trial. Defense attorneys argued that Cimbelli, who is charged with four murders, as well as conspiracy, extortion, and various other crimes related to labor payoffs, is mentally unfit to stand trial..."

In the lobby, Jane Bridger was pacing the hardwood floors and scowling at the news blaring from the old-fashioned radio. The oversize, defiantly orange sweater she wore made for an interesting contrast with her red hair and brightened the dark room with its faded furnishings.

Spotting them, she demanded, "Have you two any idea where Tiny is? There's a monsoon coming our way, and my windows are already leaking."

"He was headed downstairs fifteen minutes ago," Foster said. "Maybe you missed him."

"Not possible. I've been waiting here for twenty minutes trying to catch him."

"That's weird," Foster said. "He showed us Watson's rooms and then…"

He looked at Nick, who said, "It wasn't my turn to watch him."

Jane protested, "But where could he be? You're sure he's not still up there?"

"We've been back and forth between floors about a dozen times. We'd have seen him."

"He probably took off early," Nick said.

"He didn't leave through the front door, then," Jane Bridger said.

"So he went out the back."

"If that's the case, he's going to drag his butt back again," Jane said. "The wallpaper in my apartment is starting to peel."

"Maybe he's downstairs," Foster suggested.

Talk about a tempest in a teapot, as Nick's granny used to say. Foster seemed content to stand there with the Bridger dame discussing all the possible places Tiny could have disappeared; Nick lost patience and peeled off, heading for MacQueen's fortress. He relieved his general annoyance by pounding heavily on the scratched door, although he doubted if even those blows could be heard over the blasting TV.

Behind him he could hear Bridger saying, "He's a freak. I'm all for handi-capable, but there's a limit. Remember when he tried to keep that rat in a cage in the basement? A pet rat! And MacQueen's so-called dogs kept going after it? I think the rat was bigger than both dogs put together."

"He was talking about ghosts today," Foster said.

"Ghosts! I've heard that from him too. I think he gets it from David. Mr. Center. You know he — Mr. Center — claims he only moved here because the place is haunted."

"Haunted by who?"

"I don't know. Some Indian princess or a colonial milkmaid or something."

"A milkmaid?"

"I don't remember the details. The place was originally a farm or something, wasn't it?"

"Tiny said the ghost wore yellow socks, like the man in my bathtub."

"I never saw a milkmaid with yellow socks."

"I never saw a milkmaid."

MacQueen's door opened abruptly, catching Nick off guard.

"You again!" she accused around a cigarette. "Can't I have a minute's peace?"

Nick regrouped fast. "Why didn't you mention Tiny's keys were stolen?"

If he'd thought to catch her off guard, he was disappointed. "They weren't stolen! They were lost. For a day. You know how many times that damn retard has lost his keys?" She was giving

herself a home permanent, and the place reeked like sulfur —
and she, an imp from hell in that lime green pantsuit.

"The security of every apartment in this building has been
compromised. You don't think you have a responsibility to
change   the   locks   on   your   tenants'   doors?"

She screeched, "*Change the locks!* You know how much
money that would take? More than I've got, unless you all want
a big fat rent hike."

Don't get mad, Nick warned himself. *If everything goes right in
L.A., you'll be bailing in a couple of weeks anyway.*

"I'm calling a locksmith now," he told her, "And I expect to
be reimbursed."

"Sailor, you've got a hell of a nerve!"

Something that resembled a fringed throw pillow bolted out
the door. MacQueen shrieked, "Catch it! Don't let it get away!"

"Get it yourself!" Nick snapped, all out of whatever good
manners he might have had at the weekend's start.

Foster sneezed violently as the dog veered in. It was left to
Jane to scoop it up and hand it over to MacQueen, who
snatched it without a word of thanks, withdrawing and
slamming shut her door all in one choreographed move.

"Let's call the locksmith," Nick told Foster. "We'll have him
do both rooms while he's here."

Foster sneezed again and rubbed his nose.

"I'll split the cost with you," Jane jumped in. "We'll make it
a threesome." She gave Nick a sly smile.

§ § § §

"Maybe   we   should   call   the   police,"   Foster   said,
accompanying Nick back upstairs. He had that breathy voice
again, a voice that was like fingernails on a blackboard to Nick.

"Why's that?" he asked shortly.

"Maybe they'll believe me now about the dead man and
about people getting in my rooms."

"Maybe."

"You don't think so?"

"It's not like you have the body for evidence."

Foster fell silent, considering that.

On the second-floor landing, he stopped and said, "Well, I guess I'll see you when you get back."

Not if I see you first, Nick thought. He said, "Yeah, I guess so."

"Good luck in L.A. with everything."

"Thanks."

Foster had a very straight nose, a sensitive mouth, and long eyelashes. The childlike lashes threw tender shadows across his cheekbones. They swept up and he studied Nick gravely.

Neither moved, and then Nick shocked himself by saying, "Take care of yourself."

Perry's mouth curved. "I will."

"Okay." Still Nick hesitated, but there really wasn't anything left to say.

He continued up the stairs, hearing the door to the Watson apartment close quietly behind Foster.

CHAPTER FIVE

The day was fading to dusk as Perry watched Nick's white pickup drive away.

It was dumb to feel so…let down. He barely knew Nick, after all. And what he did know was enough to warn him that he was probably maxing out the other man's patience.

The house seemed too quiet after the sound of the truck's engine died out. From the second-story window of Watson's apartment, Perry stared out at the orchard of trees, flame bright against the slate sky. Mist rose from the damp ground and slithered like a ghost snake through the woods.

Anyway, it wasn't like there was any actual danger. The house was kind of spooky, kind of creepy, but it had always been so.

He spotted someone moving through the overgrown garden below. The small figure looked like a child, but Perry recognized the pink parka and polka-dot ski cap.

Miss Dembecki?

Something in the elderly woman's furtive movements caught his attention, roused his suspicion, and because he had nothing else to do — because he needed something to take his mind off his troubles — Perry grabbed his jacket and hurried downstairs.

Jane and Mr. Teagle were hanging bedraggled garland on the staircase banister. Mr. Teagle was complaining about the Democrats Who Stole Christmas, and Jane, in a rare, indulgent mood, was egging him on.

"What was the best Christmas gift you ever got, Mr. Teagle?"

"Well, when I was a boy we didn't have a lot of money. Not like these kids today…"

Neither of them paid Perry any mind as he slipped out the back entrance leading onto the abandoned garden. The wind yanked the door from his grasp, and it banged back against the house. He waited to see if the sound alarmed his quarry, but Miss Dembecki rustled on through the overgrown ferns and weeds like a pink mole. She seemed to know her way through the muddy grounds pretty well, but then, as far as he could tell she had lived on the Alston Estate for pretty much forever.

As Perry followed Miss Dembecki, it occurred to him that he was behaving more suspiciously than she was. What did he think he was doing, spying on an old lady? What did he think he was going to find out? What dark secrets could she have? Maybe she had planted a secret tomato garden or was visiting the grave of her dead parakeet.

Still...there was something in the secretive, furtive way she was moving through the trees — and things were so weird right now. Perry automatically sped up, trying to move quietly through the wet bushes without getting too close to his quarry.

Pausing behind a stand of sugar maples, he peered into a shadowy darkness that smelled of wet earth and mold. He could hear Miss Dembecki, the sinister senior citizen, several yards ahead, crunching through the dead leaves.

Not far off, he could hear the rush of the river. The gazebo, he thought suddenly. She was heading for the gazebo. Why? Was she meeting someone? A twig cracked under his foot. He crouched down behind a dead tree stump.

Cautiously he peered around the stump.

Miss Dembecki had stopped and was looking around apprehensively. Perry ducked back, waiting, covering his mouth with his hand in case the smoke of his breath in the frosty air gave him away.

Long moments passed. Perry waited while the knees of his Levi's grew soaked. A few inches from his nose, ants crawled sluggishly in and out of the dead bark.

There came the squawk of rusty hinges and the bang of a wooden door. Peeking out, he saw that Miss Dembecki had vanished inside the gazebo.

Great. Now what? It would be difficult to cross the clearing to the gazebo without being seen from one or another of the windows. His gaze fell on a nearby birch tree, yellow branches spreading over the octagonal building.

Keeping to the cover of wild rose bushes, Perry sneaked over to the tree and climbed up into the branches, shoes slipping on the pale bark, then finding purchase.

From his perch he had an unobstructed line of vision through the grimy gazebo windows. A dull beam of light played slowly over the gently angled room.

More than this it was impossible to see in the gloom. What the heck could she be doing in there? Perry strained to hear, but that was also impossible over the distant rush of the river, the leaves whipping in the chilly breeze.

Minutes crawled by.

Was she hiding something? It would hardly take this long. And if she was looking for something…well, same argument, really. After all, she had lived on the estate for years. For what could she be searching for twenty minutes that she hadn't had plenty of time to find in the past decade or so?

Perry's hands grew numb with cold. His leg was falling asleep. He was trying to think if he had ever been more miserable in his life when the rain started again, trickling down the back of his neck. He began to worry about the cold and damp aggravating his asthma — not something Sam Spade ever had to put up with.

He massaged his leg absently, watching the wan light traveling listlessly around the room once more. Maybe he should risk climbing down and try peering through a window on the ground level. Or maybe he could just walk in and pretend to be surprised to find Miss Dembecki there — see how she reacted?

The door below him banged open, and Miss Dembecki exited the building, startling Perry — almost literally — out of his tree.

He steadied himself. Through the lattice of leaves he watched the gnomelike figure of Miss Dembecki hurrying away. He could see that she held something in one hand, but he was pretty sure it was her flashlight.

Perry let several minutes elapse. No one else left the gazebo, so he had guessed right. Not a meeting; Miss Dembecki had been looking for something.

What?

Who would use an abandoned building as a hiding place? Why?

Letting himself down gingerly through the tangle of twigs and branches, Perry dropped to the wet ground. He went into the gazebo.

It was small. The eight windows were brown with years of dirt, the wooden floor layered with dust and evidence of bird and squirrels. Perry pulled out a clean handkerchief to cover his mouth and nose.

Circling the room, he had to admit there was a conspicuous lack of hiding places — some old rattan furniture, the faded cushions ripped open long ago. That was about it.

No loose plank squeaked beneath his foot. He knocked on the walls, but they felt and sounded solid enough.

After ten minutes or so, Perry gave up and returned to the house.

§ § § §

The house was listening.

Waiting.

Perry could feel it in the silence beyond the cheerful canned laughter of *Scooby-Doo*. He sat on the late Mr. Watson's long black leather sofa eating a bowl of cereal and watching Watson's television.

Every now and then, he reassured himself with a glance over at the shiny new locks on the doors. Serious locks. Heavy-duty locks. No one was coming in through that door — unless they broke the door down. He held the only keys; he had instructed the locksmith to cut a dummy key, and he'd handed that over to Mrs. MacQueen.

So he was perfectly safe. Perfectly secure. And yet he couldn't quite shake the feeling that he was not alone.

That he was being watched.

The house was quiet. Too quiet. Up in the isolated tower rooms that hush was normal; here on the second floor Perry expected signs of life. Where was the homey scent of dinners cooking? Where was the comfortable rattle and bang of activity from any of the surrounding rooms? From the sound of things, he could be the only person on this floor or in the whole house.

Finishing a second bowl of cereal, he dumped his dish in the sink and made another nervous circuit of Watson's rooms. He almost wished he were back with his own belongings in his own familiar surroundings — except he'd never be able to use the bathroom in his apartment again.

He checked the wine rack next to Watson's stereo: lots of merlots and cabernets. Familiar brands, mostly from California. Nothing imported or priceless as far as he could tell. Not that he was any expert; he wasn't much of a drinker. Red wine usually gave him a headache, and white wine — according to his pop — was for sissies. His own cupboards were bare even if he felt like braving the deserted third floor. So why not? Watson wouldn't care, and the unknown relatives surely wouldn't miss one bottle of wine? He could leave money for the bottle on the counter.

He went into the bathroom, scrubbed down Watson's tub, then uncorked a bottle of cabernet while the bath water ran.

Two glasses of Salmon Creek and a long, hot soak went a long way toward relaxing him, and by the time Perry heaved himself out of the tub, he felt pleasantly limp and woozy.

Pulling back the covers of the freshly made bed, he crawled between the sheets. Watson had an electric blanket. Perry turned the heat up.

He thumbed through one of the comic books stacked beside the bed. More scantily clad ladies, this time fighting space aliens.

He checked the date on the magazine cover. September 1950. Watson must have collected comic books.

You could never tell about people. The few times Perry had talked to Watson, he had stuck strictly to sports and the stock market — neither topics of great interest to Perry. Whereas he'd have been fascinated to hear about these comics and graphic novels. He loved the artwork, even if half-naked ladies were not really his thing.

Curiously he turned back to the intergalactic warfare.

After a time the breasts and word balloons all blurred together. He reached up and snapped off the light.

§ § § §

What woke him? He wasn't sure. For a minute, Perry lay there in the unfamiliar darkness trying to reorient.

From next to the bed he heard the soft click of luminous numbers turning over. From the living room came the tick-tock of the clock. Closer was the scratch of tree branches against the window. Identified, he could dismiss these sounds. But there was still something….

Then he heard it. A strange sound, like…brushing. No, more like someone dragging a heavy weight down the hallway.

Throwing back the covers, he stumbled through the dark to the front door and peered out the peephole. He had a bird's-eye view of discolored carpet, somber paneling, light that had a bleached, aged quality. Even the dust motes looked old.

The hall was empty.

He listened tensely. The sound seemed to have stopped.

Perry stood shivering a few minutes longer, then gave it up and returned to his still-warm sheets.

Slowly the adrenaline drained and he sank into a velvety darkness — only to start awake as something bumped against the wall of the bedroom.

"Who's there?" he called.

Silence. That listening silence he was coming to recognize.

Perry turned on the bedside lamp.

The room seemed all deep corners and dark shadows.

His glance fell on the detective novels he had brought down from his room. A snarling man in a fedora faced down a trio of goons. The man in the fedora looked vaguely like Nick. *Don't be a dweeb*, Perry told himself. *What would Nick do in this situation?*

Nick would go check it out.

Perry considered this glumly. He cheered up when it occurred to him that more likely Nick would tell him the noise was all in his imagination and to go back to sleep.

He turned off the lamp and listened.

Nothing.

Maybe he *had* dreamed it.

He turned on his side. Slowly he drifted out on the tide.

When the dragging noises began again, Perry was too deeply asleep to hear.

§ § § § §

Monday afternoon found Perry sitting in a small room at the *Fox Run Gazette* studying the projected images from pages of back issues as they appeared and disappeared on the dingy walls.

NEGRO STUDENTS SIT AT WOOLWORTH LUNCH COUNTER read the headline for the February 2, 1960 issue of the *Gazette*.

Perry sighed. He clicked the projector. He had nothing else to do. He was officially on vacation with nowhere to go. The dream he had centered his life around for the past months was over. The memory of those imagined Sunday brunches and walks along the beach, the anticipated trips to museums and art galleries…recalling those treasured fantasies was even more painful than the humiliating reality.

Which was saying something.

In fact, he had never felt less like a holiday. He couldn't even work up enthusiasm for painting — the one refuge that had never before failed him. He was too anxious to work. Too uneasy. Between Marcel and his overstrained finances...he needed something to occupy his mind, and in a weird way, the eerie occurrences at the estate provided a useful distraction.

Jane had dropped by his room for breakfast that morning. Ostensibly, she was there to borrow a cup of milk, but he suspected she thought he needed cheering up. Actually, maybe Jane was the one who needed cheering up, because once settled on his sofa she had seemed to have nothing to say, restlessly surfing the TV channels with the remote control.

"Aren't you going to work today?" he asked, surprised. He'd never known Jane to call in sick to the realtor's office where she worked.

She lifted a negligent shoulder. "They can do without me for a day or two. I don't like the look of those clouds. I'd hate to get stranded on the other side of the bridge. In fact, if I were you, I'd think twice about going into town if you don't have to."

She did have a point. The bridge occasionally flooded out, but the idea of sitting around in Watson's rooms all day...no thanks. He'd prefer sleeping in his car.

Watching Jane impatiently clicking buttons on the remote, he asked on impulse, "Did you ever hear of the ghost of Witch Hollow?"

Jane tore her gaze away from truTV. "Ghosts before lunchtime? Oh, sweetie!"

"But didn't you tell me something about this place being haunted?"

"How irresponsible of me," Jane murmured. "You don't believe everything I tell you, do you?"

"About a third."

Jane laughed. "Smart kid." She pressed the remote control again, and a channel blasted Christmas gift ideas as it flashed by. She glanced at Perry. "I seem to recall reading something in the newspaper last year. One of those local color articles," she admitted.

"It specifically mentioned the Alston Estate?"

Jane squinted as though she were looking into the distant past. Or perhaps she had a hangover. She didn't look well, now that he noticed. Maybe she was ill but just couldn't admit to needing a sick day. There were people like that; tiresome people who made a crusade out of never calling in sick and then infecting all their coworkers with the plague. Perry was sensitive to this, being one of those people who always caught whatever plague was circulating.

"I want to say yes," Jane mused. "It was back in the twenties. Or maybe it was the forties. There was a murder or something. But it's an old house; naturally, there's history."

"I never heard about any murder," Perry said doubtfully.

"MacQueen's hush-hush about it. Afraid it will scare prospective tenants, I guess. You know the older generation."

If Mrs. Mac was anything to go by, the older generation was capable of licking the younger generation blindfolded and with one arm tied behind its back.

"It's different for people of her generation," Jane clarified. "Murder was a big scandal then."

"Right," said Perry, puzzling over the idea that murder was no longer a big scandal. "And so this ghost was the victim of a murder?"

Jane pressed the remote control again. "You'd have to check that out, sweetie. My memory's a little vague."

So that's what Perry had decided to do. Check it out. After all, he'd read enough detective novels to know nobody ever solved a mystery sitting on his butt watching the rain strip the leaves off the trees.

He pressed the projector button and another slightly fuzzy page flashed on the wall. It could take hours or even days to find what he was looking for; if it even existed. Jane's memory was notoriously faulty. He scanned the enlarged image for any mention of the Alston Estate, or any other historical homes in the area, and then squeezed the button once more.

This was dull work, but it gave him something to do. Something to think about besides Marcel.

He wondered how Nick was doing in Los Angeles. He wondered if he'd had his interview yet. He wondered if Nick would get the job and move to California.

Reaching the end of the reel, Perry rose, threaded the next strip of microfilm into the projector. Sitting down, he refocused the print on the wall and scowled at it. Detective work was a lot more interesting in the pages of authors like Dashiell Hammett and Raymond Chandler. Granted, he was just as glad that he didn't have to deal with lantern-jawed tough guys beating him to a pulp, or sloe-eyed dames trying to slip him Mickey Finns.

He pressed the button.

It was starting to look like the last event of real interest at Fox Run had been the Revolutionary War. He clicked again.

And then, just as he was getting fed up, Perry came across an article concerning the local Preservation Society's efforts to renovate homes in the area. In the same issue was a story about yuppies moving into the valley and purchasing older homes. The newspaper was about five years old.

Perry leaned forward on his elbows, reading eagerly.

> Vermont's long and colorful history can be found in the microcosm of Fox Run located in the Northeast Kingdom. Some of the area's oldest buildings are preserved for posterity on the property formerly known as the Hennesey Farm. Now part of the Alston Estate, the 18th-century farmhouse boasts an icehouse, a dovecote, and a sun porch.

Bingo, thought Perry. He began to jot down notes.

> The house was built in 1780 by Colonel Geoffrey Hennesey as a wedding present for his new bride. Hennesey, a commander in the Continental Army, died a month after the house was completed. His widow lived there

alone until her own death in 1800. The
lonely spirit of the lovely young widow is
said to confine her nocturnal ramblings to
the original structure.

Which part of the house is the original structure? wondered Perry.

During Prohibition the house sold to the
investment banker Henry Alston, who
extensively renovated the structure. The
house was the setting for many gala society
gatherings. In 1923, Alston married one of
Ziegfeld's Glorified Girls, silver-screen
legend Verity Lane, and old money met new
in a clash of Titans. Typically, most
evenings' amusements included hot jazz,
bootlegged alcohol, and illegal gambling
for the Alston's wealthy and famous
friends. The house gained notoriety during
the winter of 1932, when the notorious
gangster Shane Moran and his gang descended
on a private party, stealing over a million
dollars worth of jewels and valuables from
the wealthy partygoers.

Perry whistled soundlessly. Hard to believe the dusty, dark
halls of the old house had ever been alive with laughter and
music.

Moran was killed by G-men in a shoot-out
less than a week following the robbery. The
whereabouts of the loot remains a mystery
to this day.

Perry thought of Miss Dembecki prowling around in the
gazebo. Surely not? Moran had escaped with his loot and had
not met his violent fate till a few days later. And yet...? She had
surely been searching for something — and searching in such a
way that seemed to indicate she didn't want anyone to know she
was hunting.

Unsurprisingly, the ghost of Shane Moran
has also been said to prowl the dusty
corridors of the Alston Estate. For
information on these and other ghosts,
check out *New England's High Spirits and
Gay Ghosts.*

Perry jotted down the dates in his notebook and read the article again.

So…the house was supposedly haunted? But regardless of what David Center thought, that had been no ectoplasmic manifestation in Perry's bathtub. *Center.* Perry gave a little shiver as he thought of the other man's clammy, cold hands reaching for his.

Leaving the stuffy little room, he went out for cocoa and a quick bite at a coffee shop down the street.

He was finishing up a grilled cheese sandwich and French fries at the counter, when he noticed a big man in a blue jacket showing a photo to the waitress. The woman shook her head, and Perry glanced at the photo with casual interest. He was too far away to see anything.

The man in the blue sports coat stared idly around the diner and noticed Perry's interested gaze. His eyes narrowed, his expression hardening.

You got a problem?

He didn't need to say the words aloud. His look said it all. Perry's gaze dropped to his plate. He carefully selected a French fry as though planning to award a prize to the perfect potato wedge.

Was he a cop? Perry considered this possibility and then dismissed it. The man didn't look like a cop. He looked like an ex-football player. Nobody's nose started out in that mashed shape, and his narrow-set eyes had a mean does-not-play-well-with-others cast to them. Never mind football player, he looked like a thug — a thug with a severely underdeveloped fashion sense. His coat was as ugly as the one worn by the dead man in Perry's tub.

A light bulb went on. *Maybe he was a P.I.*

Then again, perhaps that was just a short in Perry's thought process. Though the man looked like the down-on-their-luck private eyes in the pulp novels that he loved, it was doubtful that real P.I.s looked so stereotypical. All the same, *could* there be a connection between the men in the ugly sports coats? Could this guy maybe be looking for the dead man who had disappeared out of Perry's bathtub?

Somebody must be looking for him.

Or was this all getting a little too Walter Mitty? There was no reason to believe the dead guy was either a cop or a crook. And as for the bruiser in the blue sports coat, the most likely explanation was he was a prospective buyer looking for a particular house in the area.

Anything else was pretty farfetched, right? Not everyone with criminally bad taste was a career crook. Perry turned the idea of a possible connection over in his mind while he continued to stare at his plate as though counting the remaining French fries.

At last the bruiser in the blue sports coat finished paying for his meal and let himself out the glass door with a jangle of bells. Perry turned to look through the window at the back of the out-of-towner disappearing down the tree-lined street.

"He's a long way from home," the waitress remarked to no one in particular.

"Where's he from?" Perry asked.

She shrugged. "Sounded like New York to me. Buffalo maybe?"

"What was he looking for?"

"*Who*," the waitress corrected. "Some girl who ran out on her husband. No one from around here, that's for sure."

CHAPTER SIX

Returning to the newspaper office, Perry requested microfilm dating from 1930 from the bored Asian youth behind the desk.

The kid said, as though Perry should have known this before he wasted time asking, "He's already using it."

"He who?"

With a sigh, the kid shoved the clipboard Perry's way. He read the tall, sloping letters: R. Stein.

The day was getting weirder and weirder. Mr. Stein had never struck Perry as a history buff — let alone a believer in the supernatural. The fact that he was checking out microfilm from the 1930s had to be more than a coincidence.

So maybe Perry's line of inquiry wasn't so far off?

He asked the kid, who had returned to his Game Boy, "Do you know if the hard copies of this stuff still exist?"

"You mean the old newspapers?"

"Yeah."

The kid shrugged. "Not here they don't." With a weary patience he pointed out, "That's the point of the microfilm."

"Do you know if the original copies were donated to the library? Or maybe one of the colleges?"

"Nope. No idea."

Perry thought it over. "Could you ask someone?"

"There's no one here to ask. Everyone is *busy.*" Shaking his head at the insensitivity of some people, he returned to the rescue of the heroes of Golden Sun.

Perry muttered thanks and departed. Walking across the half-empty parking lot, he tried to make sense of what he had learned. Rudy Stein was an ex-cop, so maybe there would be reason for him to check out a crime-related story, but surely the time frame put his inquiry in the more-than-suspicious-coincidence category.

But more-than-suspicious how exactly? Maybe Stein *was* a history buff. Maybe he was writing a book about the history of Fox Run. The truth was, Perry knew very little about his fellow tenants. Since he'd arrived at the Alston Estate a little over a year ago, his life had revolved around his painting and then his Internet romance with Marcel.

Stein could be writing a book about the colorful history of the area. Miss Dembecki could have been searching for a lost earring. Or perhaps they *were* both hunting for Shane Moran's missing loot.

Or maybe Perry had read too many detective novels. Maybe Stein was taking a night school course. Maybe he was curious about the ghost stories too? Maybe, being an ex-cop, his instincts were aroused? Because sure as anything, something screwy was going on at the Alston Estate.

He stopped in his tracks as he realized that Stein would have seen Perry's name on the clipboard when he went to sign out the microfilm.

Not that there was any logical reason for Perry hiding his interest in the history of the house. After his own experience he had every reason to be curious about any ghost stories concerning his current home.

All the same, Perry sort of wished no one at the estate knew he was checking into the house's past.

Since Stein's presence stymied his own investigation for the moment, he climbed back into his car and drove around the block to the library.

As he was supposed to be enjoying his preciously hoarded vacation time in San Francisco, his sudden appearance was met with universal surprise. Perry felt obliged to make up a story about sudden illness in his friend's family, and his coworkers were suitably sympathetic for a couple of minutes before being distracted by the demands of the workday. Perry was glad he hadn't confided the true romantic purpose of his trip. It was painful enough without everyone knowing he'd been dumped.

He declined the offer of rescheduling vacation for a later date and went into the back office to check his e-mail. He logged onto the staff computer with a feeling of nervous nausea.

Sure enough, there was an e-mail from Marcel.

Perry read it on the computer monitor, heart pounding, cold sweat breaking out all over his body like he was coming down with flu.

> *I'm sorry*, Marcel had written. *I don't know what else to say. I thought it was over between Gerry and me — maybe it is, but I have to give it one last chance. I hope we can still be friends. You are a special person in my life, and I know you will soon find someone as special as you.*

Perry sat there breathing slowly and quietly, oblivious to the quiet business conducted around him.

It was over. He already knew that, but somehow seeing it in black-and-white ten-point Times New Roman made it more real. He had hoped that once they recovered from the make-up sex, Marcel and Gerry would quickly see how very wrong for each other they were. But clearly this was not the case. Even now they were probably having brunch before going for a long walk on the beach and then heading over to SFMOMA.

Amazing how much pain you could feel and still keep breathing…

And suddenly Perry had had all he could take for one day. He logged off the computer, told his indifferent coworkers good-bye, and got into his car.

Twilight was falling as he drove through the woods. Usually he loved this time of the evening, the gloaming. Trees towered in inky silhouette against a sky that was coolly and mysteriously absent of color. The lineament of fiery foliage was black and ragged in the failing light.

For the first time, Perry realized just how isolated the Alston Estate was. Witch Hollow Wood separated the mansion and grounds from the nearest farm, and the village of Fox Run was twenty miles away.

Mist rose from stygian water as he drove through the long covered bridge. The car tires thumped in the funereal silence.

§ § § §

Because his thoughts had been on Marcel all day, it surprised Perry to realize that he was missing Nick as he let himself in the front door of the old house.

He wondered again if Nick would take the job in California. He couldn't imagine that he wouldn't pass the interview, whatever it was. It was hard to picture anyone more capable than Nick Reno. Of course, it didn't — shouldn't — really matter to him, one way or the other, but the thought of Nick leaving was depressing.

He closed the door and turned the deadbolt. Tattered green holiday garland wound haphazardly up the long banister. More garland draped drunkenly from the chandelier. It probably would have constituted a fire hazard, but the chandelier, like most of the original electrical fixtures did not work. Instead, ugly modern lights had been installed. They glared down on the empty room highlighting the dust, the threadbare upholstery of the battered chairs, the discarded ladder still lying next to the staircase.

From down the hall he could hear Mrs. Mac's television blaring the local evening news: traffic accidents and sports results — sometimes it was difficult to tell the difference. Lights shone beneath Jane's door, and he briefly considered stopping by for a visit.

The thought of Mr. Fluffy discouraged him, his chest tightening at the thought of all that cat hair and dander. Besides, he really didn't have the energy for small talk. He continued up the stairway, thinking that before the disastrous weekend he'd had his plans for the future to keep him company.

Now there was nothing to look forward to.

Even as the thought registered, he rejected it impatiently. He would be okay once he started painting again. It was just the house getting to him. It felt quieter, more empty than usual.

As he reached the second level, he heard someone knocking from down the hallway. Peering through the gloom, he spotted Jane, dressed in jeans and a bright blue sweater, banging on David Center's room. As though she felt his gaze, she turned and visibly jumped.

"I didn't hear you!" she said accusingly.

"Sorry. I was just going to Wat — my — apartment." He regarded her doubtfully. She seemed...agitated. Not angry exactly, but...for sure not her usual relaxed, amused self. Maybe calling in sick to work had been a mistake. The atmosphere seemed to be finally getting to her too, although Jane previously seemed impervious to atmosphere.

She gave a final smack to Center's door and asked, "Where *is* everybody?"

"Mrs. Mac's TV is on. I could hear it from the lobby."

"I meant humans," Jane retorted nastily. "I haven't seen Dembecki or Teagle. Stein has been out all day. I suppose David — Mr. Center — is still at work."

"If you call reading tarot cards work."

Jane snorted, but she didn't make the expected joke. Perry had noticed that in the past couple of weeks, Jane's attitude toward David Center had softened. Jane was so self-reliant and contained he had never considered that she might develop romantic feelings — especially for someone like David Center, whom Perry didn't like. It made him feel lonelier still.

"It pays the bills, which is more than my crap job does." Abandoning her post, Jane joined him in front of Watson's door. "God*damn* this place," she said with quiet vehemence.

"Is everything okay?" Perry asked. Clearly everything wasn't okay, but he didn't like to pry.

She shot him a sideways glance and muttered, "Yes, fine. It's this place. It gets on my nerves."

He could understand that. But this tired and tense Jane was so different from the Jane he knew. Everyone seemed different these days. Ever since Perry had returned from his aborted vacation.

Or had he just not noticed how odd everyone was in those weeks he had been happily cocooned in dreams of a future with Marcel?

Jane added, as though it was the last straw, "And Tiny has run away again. When's your new chum, G.I. Joe, due back?"

"What makes you think Tiny ran away?"

She made a disgusted sound. "He's gone. Nobody's seen him since yesterday."

Yesterday, after he had opened Watson's rooms, disposed of the dead fish, and ducked out before Jane could recruit him to fix her leaking windows? Could this be relevant to the other mysterious happenings at the house? Perry couldn't see how. "It's not the first time he's taken off," he pointed out.

"I didn't say it was unusual; I said it was annoying."

Jane followed Perry into Watson's rooms, poking curiously through the dead man's CD and DVD collection. Perry had already checked both out. Watson enjoyed film classics such as *Behind the Green Door* and the music of Bread, the Turtles, and the Bee Gees.

Jane asked, "Don't you think it's creepy staying here? It even smells creepy."

"The whole house smells creepy."

"True." Jane scrutinized the framed print of a shapely blonde nude riding a smirking dinosaur.

"It's creepier in my rooms."

Jane's gaze swiveled from the wall decor. "Sweetie, you don't still think you saw a dead man in your bathtub?" She was laughing at him, though not unkindly.

"I don't believe I saw a ghost."

"A *ghost?*" Jane looked thoughtful. "A ghost," she repeated slowly. Then, shaking off her preoccupation, she said, "So what did you do today?"

Perry shrugged. "Looked through old newspapers. Hung out at the library."

"If you're just going to hang out the library, you might as well go back to work." She was watching him curiously. He had told Jane a little about Marcel, but even Jane didn't know how much he had pinned on that virtual relationship.

He went into Watson's kitchenette and shook the box of Froot Loops cereal sitting on the counter. "Did you want some?"

"Is that your dinner?"

"Sure. Fortified with iron."

"Sweetie, you need to eat properly. This stuff is for people saving up for decoder rings." She watched Perry splash milk into a bowl. "So the California thing is all over?"

He nodded.

"I'm sorry."

Perry shrugged.

Jane wandered around, snooping absently through Watson's belongings. She said, "You should reconsider talking to David — Mr. Center. After all, this is his area of expertise. Maybe he could hold a séance."

Through a mouthful of cereal, Perry said, *"Huh?"*

"A séance," Jane repeated. "Haven't you ever seen —"

"How would a séance help me with Marcel?"

"Marcel? Oh." Jane hastily rearranged her expression. "I wasn't thinking of Marcel. I was thinking about if the house really *is* haunted..."

"But I don't think the house is haunted!"

"I do."

Perry gaped. "You *do?*"

"Sure," she said a little defiantly.

Jane had always seemed so down-to-earth. So sensible. He couldn't get over this. "*Why?*"

She said — still defensive — "I've heard things. I've seen things. Why couldn't it be a ghost?"

"Because there's no such thing?"

"You're just being close-minded." Catching his astonished expression, she seemed to change her mind about saying more, instead heading for the door. "Well, enjoy your dinner."

"You don't have to leave." He didn't particularly want to be on his own, and the idea of Jane buying into the supernatural was kind of fascinating.

Jane's smile was vague. "I'd like to hang out, but I've got some things to take care of. Nightie-night, sweetie."

She's going to try Center again, Perry thought. When had that started? Maybe it had been going on the whole time. He'd been so wrapped up in his own dreams that he hadn't noticed what was going on under his nose.

Settling in front of the entertainment center with his cereal bowl, he began flicking channels. He didn't own a television, so this was sort of a luxury. He realized with a mild sense of shock that he hadn't watched TV since he had left home nine months earlier. He settled at last on 1931's *Little Caesar.*

This film would have been made around the start of the Great Depression, around the time that Henry Alston and his Ziegfeld Girl were throwing parties for their rich society friends, while the rest of the country starved. No wonder gangsters like Shane Moran weren't always viewed as the bad guys.

Absorbed, Perry watched the rise and fall of Rico Bandello as though it were history, laughing aloud as Edward G. Robinson snarled, "Yeah, that's what I get for liking a guy too much!"

By the time Rico ended in a hail of bullets, Perry was feeling a lot more cheerful. He decided he could use a little fresh air before turning in for the night, and a brisk walk would help tire him out before bed. The last thing he wanted was to lie awake listening to the old house creak and crack under unseen footsteps.

Grabbing his jacket, he went downstairs, letting himself out into the moist and wintry night. High above the soggy garden, white clouds slowly transformed themselves into spectral horses and mountains and dragons, then pulled apart like cotton to show the glitter of faraway stars.

Perry wondered what the stars were like in Los Angeles — could you even see stars in the smoggy L.A. skies? He wondered why he was thinking about L.A. — and Nick — yet again. Probably because he couldn't bear to think about San Francisco and Marcel.

He followed the narrow brick path through the maze of overgrown hedges and shrubs that had turned to brambles, until the path gave way to broken steps and then dirt and mud.

The old crooked tower of the dovecote stood before him. In the insubstantial starlight it looked like a witch's house. It was one of his favorite subjects. He had made several sketches of it and painted it twice — even selling one of the paintings. He considered the structure.

It was a pretty good hiding place, really, that relatively small cylindrical tower with its interior walls made up of *boulins* or pigeonholes — assuming someone didn't have allergies or asthma. Just the idea of that dank darkness made his chest tighten uncomfortably.

But there was no reason to believe Shane Moran and his gang would have dumped their ill-gotten gains before escaping into the woods — what sense would that make?

The bushes rustled behind him, and he whirled, heart pounding in terror. When his eyes verified that there *was*, in fact, someone standing there — a bulky black shape in the darkness — he thought he might actually faint.

"What the hell are you doing out here?" Rudy Stein demanded. He sounded as shaken as Perry felt.

Perry's heart resumed beating as he recognized the other man. "Walking."

Stein said aggressively, trying to cover his own fright, "Funny time for a walk, if you ask me!"

Perry squared his shoulders. "I could say the same to you."

There was surprised quality to Stein's silence. At last he gave a funny laugh. "Yeah, well, you better watch your step," he said, pointing downward.

Perry looked down and realized he was standing in a puddle.

Stein gave another of those curt laughs. "Have a good night," he said, and strode off in the direction of the river.

Perry gazed after him, but Stein's figure was soon swallowed by the shadows.

The night closed around him again and he shivered. That was enough fresh air for one evening.

He made his way back to the house, went up to Watson's rooms — again conscious of the strained silence within the empty halls — and prepared for bed.

Flossing his teeth, Perry weighed his options for the next day. Running into Stein seemed to confirm his suspicion that something was going on in the old house, and while it wasn't really his business, the fact that a dead body had been dumped in his bathtub did sort of elicit his interest.

He decided to visit the historical society the next day and see what he could find on the house. He could try church records too. They were always useful in detective novels, although he wasn't sure what he would be looking for in this case. Records of births and deaths would be the usual thing; perhaps Shane Moran had been a local boy. That would give him possible ideas for where Moran might have stashed his loot.

Perry blinked sleepily at the turn his thoughts had taken.

Shane Moran's loot? He wasn't planning to spend the rest of his vacation treasure hunting, was he? How had he gone from curiosity about the history of the house to wondering about Shane Moran's final heist?

He rinsed and spat water into the sink, turned off the taps, and returned to the unfamiliar bedroom, climbing into the enormous bed. He turned on the electric blanket, snapped out the light and stared up at the ceiling. Shadows flicked across the pale surface as the tree branches outside the house were shaken by gusts of wind.

The next storm front was moving in fast.

For a time he lay in the darkness, listening to the wind and the old house creaking and settling for the night.

Inevitably his thoughts turned to Marcel — Marcel who had probably not given *him* another thought since e-mailing that apologetic farewell. How could he have been so wrong about Marcel? He had believed they truly knew each other, believed that they might even know each other *better* because their exchanges were unencumbered by anything physical. Their communications were the open, honest outpourings of mind and heart. For months they had shared everything — from the most mundane things to the most deeply personal. He knew that Marcel felt that he was being sexually discriminated against at work and that he disliked his female "harridan" boss; that he was allergic to shellfish and ragweed; that he loved the apple-raisin bagels at the bakery around the corner but didn't eat them often because he gained weight easily; that he had been seventeen the first time he'd had sex with a man.

Perry was an expert in all things Marcel. But he hadn't known the most important thing: that Marcel was still in love with Gerry.

It wasn't just the embarrassment of all the things he had revealed to Marcel — all those confidences made in the belief that they shared an intimacy unique to them. He had told Marcel things he hadn't shared with anyone before. Nor was it the realization that he had been a fool — though that hurt plenty.

He was grieving — truly grieving — for the death of that dream. Sometimes holding fast to that dream had been all that kept him afloat. And now it was gone: that foolish little fantasy of cozy domesticity, himself and Marcel living together. It was almost too painful to contemplate now, those snapshots that had previously brought such comfort and joy: grocery shopping together at Whole Foods, brushing against each other in their too-small kitchen as they prepared their wonderful gourmet meals, waking up together…smiling into each other's eyes as they turned to make love…

He had known from the photos that Marcel would be good-looking, and he was. Tall and boyish, maybe a little plump — but in a cute way — unruly brown hair. True, his hair was thinner in real life, and Marcel had been a little bit older than his photo. He had bright blue eyes — a very different blue from the somber blue of Nick Reno's. Perry had known he was going to love Marcel from the minute he saw him waiting at the gate looking apologetic and sheepish, in his own good-looking rumpled way.

Perry stared at the Armando Drechsler posters of Mayan princesses and tribal dancers on Watson's bedroom wall. In the moonlight they looked like giant tarot cards, or travel posters to a mysterious unknown.

It was over now. And though he knew it was silly and melodramatic, Perry felt like his life was over too. He was never going to find anyone. He would live out his days at the Alston Estate just like little Miss Dembecki, until he became one of its ghosts too.

§ § § §

Click. Click. The alarm clock turned over the glowing green numerals of 12:01 a.m. Perry opened his eyes.

Where was he? And then he remembered. He was staying in Mr. Watson's apartment.

He was drowsily taking stock, deciding if he needed to pee badly enough to make that trip across the unheated room, when he heard it: a low moan.

What the…?

He had to have misheard. Or imagined it entirely. His ears strained the silence.

Nothing but the beat of blood rushing in his ears.

He continued to listen alertly.

He wished he hadn't awakened. Now he was alive to the sounds of the house: the strange squeaks like floorboards under uncertain feet, the sigh of the wind down the chimney like a whispering voice.

He could imagine what Nick would say of such imaginings. The thought of Nick bolstered his sagging courage. Nick did not believe in ghosts and neither did Perry.

Of course, if some human agent was standing outside his room making spooky noises, it wasn't so reassuring. Was someone trying to scare him into leaving the Alston Estate?

All they had to do was ask.

Well, not really. He didn't have any place else to go, and few places were as cheap to rent as his rooms in the isolated old house. And he wasn't actually *that* chicken, although he knew no one was ever going to mix him up for a tough guy.

Something moved inside the closet.

Perry went rigid. He told himself it was his imagination.

But then the closet door banged as though someone kicked it. Perry sat bolt upright. He fumbled for the lamp, knocking the clock off the stand.

Scrambling out of bed, his foot tangled in the sheet, and he nearly fell. His eyes never left the white, motionless closet door.

On his feet he reached the closet. His chest rose and fell, his hand shook, and yet something made him reach out, fingers brushing the glass knob.

He yanked open the door.

CHAPTER SEVEN

Nick tossed back the rest of his Seven and Seven and handed the plastic cup to the flight attendant as she bumped down the aisle, trash bag in hand. She smiled at him, and Nick gave her a wide, meaningless grin in return.

I must be nuts, he thought, staring out at the black slate of night sky out the little square window.

Roscoe had wanted him to stay and celebrate — and finally he had something to celebrate. After Marie, after his discharge, after the monotony of civilian life with no job, no prospects, finally there was something to celebrate.

And what did Nick do? He grabbed the first available plane back for Vermont — which he hated anyway and couldn't wait to put behind him once and for all. What the hell was the matter with him?

But he kept thinking of the Foster kid. Perry. There was something not kosher at the estate, and that fragile boy was not equipped to deal with it. Not that it was Nick's problem — although he was now officially in the P.I. business. Well, soon. After he finished his training.

All around him on the crowded aircraft, other passengers were settling down for sleeping or reading. Nick stretched his long legs out as far as he could beneath the seat in front of him — which wasn't far. He'd have liked to get up and move around, but there was a woman with a baby in the aisle seat, and he'd have preferred public flogging to the risk of waking that shrieking mouth again. It was amazing the lung power in something that small.

He resettled in his seat, trying to get more comfortable, and glanced at his watch. Another two hours before they landed. He'd have to waste another hour going through baggage claim and finding his truck, and then another hour back to the Kingdom. He sighed and closed his eyes. Might as well get some rest. It would be after midnight before he made it back to Creepsville.

§ § § §

There was a fire truck parked outside the Alston mansion when Nick pulled up. Sheriff's department cars were angled along the drive and grass. Blue and red lights cut through the misty night like lasers. An ambulance was parked a few feet from the front door.

Nick got out of his pickup, shrugging into his leather jacket. The unease that had dogged him since he'd left the estate bloomed into full consternation.

He strode across the rain-slicked grass. A deputy sheriff tried to stop him. Nick brushed past with a curt word of explanation. His heart was thumping unpleasantly; chill premonition slithered down his spine.

In the drafty front hall, the residents had all gathered in their nightclothes — that motley collection of pajamas and dressing gowns in which people always dressed for disaster.

"What's happened?" he demanded.

A gray-faced Mrs. MacQueen, looking more like James Cagney than ever in a thick plaid wool robe and men's style slippers, shook her head.

He looked at the others. Stein was nervously chewing the inside of his cheek. Teagle sat in a chair next to the unlit fireplace, his head shaking, his big, hands white beneath the freckles. That walking cadaver, David Center, stood next to the Bridger woman, his bony hand fastened on the emerald sleeve of her kimono-clad arm. Bridger looked stoic, but Nick knew her type. The sky could be falling; she wouldn't panic easily.

Paramedics appeared on the second level, wheeling a gurney. The figure on the gurney was covered.

Miss Dembecki whispered, "Perry."

The world seemed to stop.

Nick had to clear his throat to speak. His voice came out funny and raspy. "Perry's dead?"

So his hunch had been right. Trouble. Bad trouble.

Jane Bridger broke in. "Perry's not dead! What are you saying, Miss Dembecki? That's *Tiny*. Perry found Tiny dead in Watson's bedroom closet."

"Tiny?" Miss Dembecki murmured bewilderedly. She looked around the circle of watching faces. "But then...?"

The gurney and the EMTs were making their precarious way down the narrow stairs, banging loudly against the banister. Tiny's heavy carcass was no easy load.

"Where's Perry?" Nick demanded of Jane.

She tore her gaze from the grim sight on the staircase. "Upstairs being questioned, I guess."

Nick waited until the EMTs had made it safely to the bottom, then he took the stairs two at a time.

A deputy stopped him outside Watson's apartment. Through the open door he could see Perry talking to an older man in uniform. The sheriff? Perry was seated on the low sofa. He wore jeans and a striped pajama top, his pale hair sticking up in bed-head tufts. He was speaking in voice so low that Nick couldn't hear what was said. He could see the kid was gripping his inhaler.

"Listen, you'll have to go back downstairs with the others," the deputy warned.

Nick considered it, while the deputy bristled. There didn't seem anything to be gained by insisting on staying — Perry looked shaken but unharmed, and it was doubtful even the local police were dumb enough to think he was a suspect in a homicide.

Nick returned downstairs to wait with the others.

"Just what the hell's going on up there?" MacQueen demanded, huddled in the chair on the other side of the fireplace. "*Shut up!*" she screamed suddenly.

There was an astonished silence, and then from down the hall came the sound of her mutts whining and scratching at the closed door of her apartment.

"Are they still questioning Perry?" Jane Bridger asked after a polite few seconds' pause.

"It looked like it."

"It doesn't make sense," David Center said worriedly. "The spirits would not harm a simple soul like Tiny."

Speaking of simple souls. Nick studied him bleakly. Center wore an incredible dressing gown of paisley blue and purple, proving, in Nick's opinion, that he really was blind.

Bridger patted Center's hand in absent reassurance.

"Well, I'm going back to bed," Mrs. MacQueen announced, heaving herself to her feet.

Stein laughed. "Good luck with that."

"Ma'am, the sheriff will want to question everyone in the house," the deputy stationed at the front door said.

"Then he can wake me up!" Mrs. MacQueen swaggered off, and the deputy looked around helplessly before following her down the hall.

Perry appeared at the top of the landing. "They want you, Janie," he said hollowly.

"Me? Why am *I* next?" Bridger protested, and it was Center's turn to soothe her with murmurs and hand pats.

"They'll want to talk to everyone," Stein said knowledgeably, and Dembecki began twittering anxiously.

Muttering under her breath, Jane went up the stairs, silk dressing gown whispering, passing Perry on his way down.

Nick was disconcerted at the flip his heart did as Perry's heavy eyes met his. *Just relief that the kid's okay*, he told himself. He'd have felt guilty as hell if something had happened to Foster on what should have been his watch.

Perry came to stand next to him. "You're back." He greeted Nick wanly and managed a twitchy smile.

Nick nodded curtly. "How are you doing?"

"Okay." He turned the Bambi eyes on Nick. "They said I could go back to my rooms. *My* rooms. They're sealing Watson's apartment." He swallowed hard.

"You can stay with me," Nick said. Perry seemed to work to keep his expression stoic, but the ardent gratitude was right below the surface, and if they'd been alone Nick would probably have done something unwise like put an arm around those slender shoulders.

The deputy came back. "That dame has lost her marbles," he announced.

"No argument here," Stein said, and Teagle shook off his white-faced preoccupation long enough to make a disapproving noise.

Dembecki twittered some more. Nick wouldn't have been surprised to see her take flight right out of this cuckoo's nest.

To the deputy, he said, "I've been away for forty-eight hours. Am I a suspect or can I go to bed?"

"Sheriff wants to talk to everyone that lives here."

Nick handed Perry his keys. "Get some rest."

Without a word, Perry took the keys and disappeared up the staircase.

Nick watched him go — tight little ass and those long, coltish jeans-clad legs — till Perry vanished around the bend in the staircase.

He leaned back against the wall to wait, unobtrusively watching the others. Jane Bridger came down in a worse temper than she'd been in when she'd gone up. David Center was next. Bridger volunteered to escort him, but he declined brusquely.

Bridger retreated huffily to her own quarters.

Shortly afterward, Nick's name was called.

He found the sheriff in Watson's quarters. Sheriff Butler was a short, lean man with a neat silver mustache and piercing green eyes. Nick put him in the fifty-five to sixty-five range; he was the type who aged well.

"Ex-Navy SEAL, huh? That's a pretty tough outfit."

Nick's eyes narrowed. This could go a couple of ways. Some guys admired the dedication and discipline required to be a SEAL. Some guys were intimidated by it and tried to prove otherwise.

Indicating that Nick should sit, Butler proceeded to ask his name, age, occupation, flight details, and purpose of his recent trip before really getting down to it.

"So if I understand you correctly, Mr. Reno, you've been out of town since" — he didn't have to check his notes — "Sunday the eighth."

Nick said crisply, "You understand correctly."

"When was the last time you saw Jasper Bryant?"

"Who?"

"The handyman. Tiny."

"Sunday morning. He let us, Perry Foster and me, into these rooms."

"And?"

"And what? He took some dead fish out of the fish tank and he left. I haven't seen him since."

"Where did he go when he left this apartment?"

Nick said shortly, "You must have me confused with the psychic next door." He glanced at the sheriff's notes — Butler kept track in tiny, dark script that could have been printed by a machine. "I have no idea what he did after he left here. I take it he didn't die from natural causes?"

"He was shot to death."

Nick thought of the .45 caliber pistol taped — hopefully still taped — to the wall in the cupboard beneath his kitchen sink "He wasn't shot to death in this apartment, I'll tell you that right now. He sure as hell wasn't in the closet when I left here."

"You know that for a fact, do you?"

"Yeah, I do. I helped the kid carry some things down from his rooms. He hung a couple of shirts in the bedroom closet. I watched him. There was nothing in that closet but clothes and shoes and comic books."

"How'd you know the deceased was found in the bedroom closet?"

"The Bridger woman mentioned it." Nick met the sheriff's bright gaze. He said dryly, "No way do you think that kid knowingly spent the night in this apartment with a corpse in the closet."

The sheriff's thin mouth pursed in something that might have been sour humor. "It doesn't seem likely."

Nick was silent, thinking about Tiny's comments about the ghost with yellow socks — thinking about those lost keys. The sheriff was watching him carefully.

"You got a theory?" he asked.

Nick said, "I'm sure Foster told you about the body he found in the bathtub."

"We all heard about the body in the bathtub," the sheriff said grimly.

"Maybe now you'll believe it."

Butler grimaced. "I don't see that there's automatically a connection between this homicide and the kid's story."

"Maybe not," Nick said. "But your victim was blabbing about the ghost with yellow socks shortly before someone decided to take him out."

The sheriff inspected him with those gleaming eyes. "You don't say so," he said finally.

"The kid must have told you this."

The sheriff sighed. "Yeah, he said something along those lines and offered some garbled story about missing sets of keys. But I don't know how reliable a witness he is." He raised his eyebrows. "He's a little light in the loafers, if you know what I mean."

"You're kidding," Nick drawled. "What I noticed is he's got a good eye for detail. He's a painter. He notices things."

"Maybe," Sheriff Butler said, unconvinced. "The thing is, it's the handyman who turned up dead. There's still no sign of this body from the bathtub."

When Nick didn't respond, the sheriff added, "Thanks, Reno. If we have more questions we'll contact you. Meantime, do me a favor and don't leave town without letting us know."

§ § § § §

Perry was sacked out on the sofa when Nick opened the door to his apartment, but he sat up, hair on end, eyes heavy-lidded.

"Nick?"

"You expecting someone else?"

Perry gave a little chuckle and rubbed his eyes. "I didn't think they'd keep you that long."

Nick headed for the kitchen. "Want a drink?"

"Oh. I already brushed my teeth…"

Nick rolled his eyes and took a beer from the fridge. He was staring out over the sink, drinking, when Perry's reflection appeared in the black window — a slightly rumpled ghost drifting up behind him.

"I'm glad you're back," Perry said. "And not just because I'd rather sleep in the gazebo than my own apartment."

Nick jerked his head in the direction of the fridge. "Help yourself."

Perry padded barefoot over to the fridge — and Nick resisted the temptation to tell him to put socks on his feet. He'd never considered himself the paternal type, but…someone needed to look after this boy. Once again he wondered what had gone wrong with the friend in San Francisco.

Perry got a beer, found the opener, and uncapped the bottle. He studied the design on the cap, frowning, then took a swig of beer.

"So what happened?" Nick questioned. "You found Tiny in Watson's closet?"

"That's pretty much it, yeah. I heard this weird sound. And then kind of a thump. I opened the closet and…he fell out."

Nick glanced over. Perry's fingers were white on the bottle cap, his eyes focused on whatever he had seen in Watson's closet. It had to have taken a hell of a lot of courage to open that door. Against his will, Nick was impressed. Of course, the sensible thing to do would have been run for help.

Not that there were many places to find it in this lunatic asylum.

"We both saw him leave the apartment Sunday," Nick said. "And you had the locks changed, so he couldn't have got back in."

"Somehow he did. We saw him leave, but no one saw him after that, remember? Jane was looking for him. He never came downstairs."

Nick swallowed beer, considering this.

"But he wasn't there the night before last," Perry said, "because I checked the closet. I mean, the door was ajar, so I shut it — but before I shut it, I glanced inside."

"Why?"

Delicate color rose in Perry's face. "Oh, you know," he said vaguely.

And Nick did know. He bit back a grin. Hopefully Foster didn't watch a lot of scary movies. "So he disappeared Sunday morning and showed up again, dead, in Watson's closet on Tuesday night?"

"Right."

"So someone murdered him and somehow — and for some unknown reason — dragged his body into Watson's apartment."

Perry said, "He wasn't dead."

Nick's gaze sharpened. "What do you mean he wasn't dead?"

"When I found him he was still alive," Perry said unsteadily. "He...died while I was waiting for the ambulance."

Nick set aside the inappropriate desire to offer comfort and focused on the business at hand. "Did he say anything? Did he say who did it?"

Perry shook his head. "He said, 'We're the good guys.'"

"*We're* the good guys? You and me? Or him and someone else?"

"He didn't specify."

"But what the hell does that mean?"

Perry shrugged.

"Sounds like a line from a bad movie."

Perry gave a tired laugh. "I know. But that's what he said. At least, that was the only thing I could make out. He said something else, but I couldn't make out the words."

"None of them? What did it sound like?"

Perry made a violent gurgling sound, and Nick nearly choked on his beer. "You're shitting me."

Perry gave that funny little smile, but said seriously, "It didn't sound like words. It was just...dying sounds."

"Yeah. Well..." Once again Nick had that totally out-of-character desire to offer comfort. If he didn't know it would be a fatal mistake to encourage the kid, he'd have...

But it *would* be a mistake — so he didn't.

Foster rubbed his eyes with his fist. "Gosh, I'm beat. I haven't slept in two nights."

Nick listened to this without hearing. He said slowly, "What I still don't understand is how someone managed to lug Tiny inside Watson's place after the locks were changed."

"Maybe there's a secret passage," Perry offered.

"Yeah, right." But as Nick considered it, his brows drew together. "Is that possible?"

"I don't know. I never heard of any hidden passages." Perry yawned, belatedly covering an inspiring glimpse of filling-free teeth and healthy tonsils.

"Are there blueprints of the house somewhere?"

Perry blinked at him like the question didn't compute.

"Go back to bed," Nick advised. "You look ready to keel over."

Perry said, "Night, then," and stumbled off to the sofa.

He was drifting off when a thought occurred. He pushed up on elbow calling, "How did your interview go?"

"Great," Nick said. "I got the job."

"Wow, that *is* great," Perry said hollowly and buried his head in the pillow.

Nick finished his beer, tossed the bottle, and headed for his own bed.

§ § § §

Perry woke and lay blinking at the blue rain shadows rippling across the ceiling. Another day in Paradise, as his pop used to say.

He stretched, and the blankets drew up, leaving his bare feet exposed to the cold. Shivering, he curled up once more. Nick kept his thermostat too low; Perry felt chilled and cramped after a night on the sofa.

Actually he couldn't remember when he'd last had a good night's sleep. Before Frisco. Before Marcel turned out to be mostly a figment of his imagination.

Rising, he found a saucepan in Nick's cupboard, filled it with water, and left it heating on the stove while he hurried across to his own apartment for a change of clothes and a tin of hot chocolate.

A glance over the banister showed him a deputy sheriff walking upstairs. He recognized him as one of the two who had shown up the night he had discovered the body in the bathtub. This was the younger man. "Abe" the senior partner had called him.

"Morning," Deputy Abe said laconically. His expression indicated he remembered Perry quite well too — and was equally unimpressed.

"Morning," returned Perry, drawing back. He'd had a vague idea of grabbing some of his things out of Watson's apartment, but that would have to wait.

Letting himself into his own rooms, he used his peak flow meter and noted the results on the asthma chart pinned to the fridge — pleased to note that despite the stress and strains of the past week, he was still safely in the green zone — grabbed clean clothes and the tin of Nestlé's Quik and dashed back to Nick's.

Nick's bedroom door was closed, Nick apparently still fathoms under after the long, nearly back-to-back trip to and from Los Angeles. Perry showered, shaved, and changed into clean Levi's and a forest green thermal Henley. He knew the color suited him; he had bought it for the vacation with Marcel. He examined himself in the mirror. Despite the uneasy night's sleep, he looked better than he had recently. But then he felt better — mostly because Nick was back.

Last night he'd been too tired to tell him what he'd learned about the house's history — last night none of it had seemed relevant — but this morning he couldn't wait to hear Nick's thoughts.

Pouring himself a cup of cocoa, he sat down at the table and glanced over the notes he'd made at the library the day before. He was still reading when Nick padded in.

Unshaven, bleary eyed, he stalked over to the gas range. "'Morning," he growled.

"Good morning," Perry said cheerfully. "There's hot water."

"I see that. I take coffee with my hot water." He scowled at Perry's mug. "Tell me those are not bunny-shaped marshmallows."

Perry blushed.

"Don't you drink coffee?" Nick sounded disbelieving. "Couldn't you at least make coffee for those of us who don't like bunnies in our morning beverage."

"I don't know how to make coffee," Perry admitted.

Nick turned that red-rimmed gaze on Perry. "You're not kidding," he said at last.

"No. I don't drink it, so I never learned."

Nick shuddered. He turned on the taps and filled the stainless coffeepot. "How'd you sleep?" he asked over the rush of water.

"Okay," Perry said, trying to repress a grin. He enjoyed Nick's company — even when Nick was feeling grouchy.

Nick finished filling the coffeepot and sat down at the table. He nodded at Perry's notes. "What are you doing?"

"I was at the newspaper morgue yesterday. I learned some things about the house."

"Like what?"

"Well, it is supposed to be haunted…" At Nick's expression he added hastily, "But that's not the interesting part."

Nick scrubbed his face with his hands. "Give me the interesting part."

He had square, capable hands. They were tanned — Nick was tanned everywhere as far as Perry could see even though it was late autumn now. He'd have liked to see if Nick was brown under those flannel shirts and jeans; he'd have liked to feel those square, capable hands on his body. He brought his thoughts up short, a little shocked at his own shallowness. Here he was, just two days after losing the love of his life, and he was fantasizing about another man.

A straight man at that.

Although…sometimes the way Nick looked at him made him wonder. Perry wasn't vastly experienced, but he did know what that certain alertness, that awareness, meant in another person's stare. It started in kindergarten and never stopped as far as he could tell.

He realized that Nick was now looking at him, waiting to be brought up to speed, and said hastily, "Back in the thirties there was a big robbery on the estate, and a bunch of jewels and money were stolen from guests by a gangster by the name of Shane Moran. No one ever found the loot."

"So what...the ghosts of the robbed guests are haunting the halls of Alston Manor?"

"No. Shane Moran is supposed to haunt the grounds. He was killed in a shoot-out in Witch Hollow Woods."

Nick groaned. "Lemme guess. He was shot for wearing a loud yellow sports jacket?"

Perry laughed. "Maybe. But the guy in my bathtub was not wearing costume dress. That coat came from Big and Tall World, I'm betting."

"The Sopranos Collection," Nick said.

"Hey." Perry looked thoughtful. "He *did* look like a gangster, sort of."

"Not everyone with a taste for checks and plaids is actually a criminal, although I can see why you might think so."

Perry laughed.

"Jesus, you're chipper in the morning," Nick complained, but he didn't seem unduly upset about it. He rose. "Eggs and bacon okay?"

Perry was considering Nick's first comment. His mother used to say he was "sunny natured," and he guessed that was true. The last few days had been spent in a fog of misery after the fiasco with Marcel, but his natural optimism was beginning to reassert itself. He was amazed to realize he had barely thought of Marcel today until this very moment.

"I guess I'm kind of a morning person," he informed Nick.

"I'll keep it in mind," Nick said. "Scrambled or fried?"

"I think I'll just have cereal."

"I don't think so," Nick said. "You need to eat real food. No wonder you have asthma."

"Asthma doesn't have anything to do with eating." Perry was slightly amused, slightly defensive.

"No? Well, I'm not a doctor, but it seems like the better shape you're in, the fewer problems you'd have with your breathing. Do you ever work out?"

"I hike a lot. In the woods."

"You need to work out," Nick informed him. "Weights. Build your muscles. You have to be able to take care of yourself in this world."

While Nick delivered his lecture on fitness, he cracked eggs, chopped onions, grated cheese. Bacon popped on the stove. Coffee perked. It was homey. Cozy. Perry warned himself not to enjoy it too much.

"Did you tell the cops about this stuff?" Nick asked.

"I didn't think of the secret passage till I was talking with you."

"Not *that*," Nick brushed aside the notion of a secret passage. "I mean the stuff about the missing jewels. That's what you think is going on here, right? Someone is looking for Shane Moran's missing loot."

He raised his eyebrows at whatever he read in Perry's face. "Kid, it wasn't that hard to follow where you were heading."

Perry couldn't help it. Nick was so damned sharp and savvy. He couldn't imagine what it was like to be someone like that. Someone who always knew what to do — and the best way to do it.

"I tried," Perry said. "The sheriff kept interrupting me and asking about Tiny."

Nick put the plate in front of Perry. "Eat up."

Perry shoved his notes aside and picked up his fork. "You're a good cook."

"My grandmother taught me to cook. She thought it was important for a man to be able to make himself a home-cooked meal when he wanted it. Thank God she did. My wife was the worst cook ever born. She made MR rations seem appetizing."

"I didn't know you were married."

"Divorced." Nick added curtly, "Got the papers Saturday."

"How long were you married?"

"Too long." His tone indicated that this topic was now off-limits.

Perry ate his breakfast silently while Nick stared out the window. The phone rang and Nick went to answer it. Perry heard him pick up, and then after a moment of silence, say curtly, "We'll be right over."

Nick stuck his head in the kitchen.

"That was Stein. He said he heard someone walking overhead in your apartment so he tried ringing. No one answered. He called here to find out if you'd moved back or not. I said we'd meet him over there."

"Why didn't he tell the deputy?"

"He said the deputy is gone."

"He's probably in my apartment." Perry's eyes widened as he watched Nick squat down, open the cupboard beneath the sink, and pull out a pistol. Nick shoved the pistol in the back waistband of his Levi's with the casualness that bespoke great familiarity with weapons. Perry's father had handled his weapons the same way.

Nick glanced at him, the lines of his face hard and businesslike. "Why would he be?"

It took Perry a second to remember his comment about the deputy. "I'm probably a suspect."

"I give the police more credit than that." And with that Nick was on his feet and out the door.

Perry pushed away from the table to follow reluctantly.

CHAPTER EIGHT

The trip from Nick's tower room to Perry's took about a minute. Reaching Perry's apartment, they found the door slightly open.

Nick pulled his gun, planted one hand in Perry's chest, and whispered, "Stay here."

Perry was happy to obey. He watched Nick start forward. Nick glanced back at him, and an expression of exasperation fleeted across his set face. He jerked his head backward, giving Perry to understand he was supposed to get out of the line of potential fire.

He plastered himself against the wall behind Nick, heart hammering hard. His chest was getting that tight, itchy feeling. *God, please not now...* He fought the desire to cough.

Nick kicked open the door and slipped inside the front room, gun at the ready. He pivoted alertly to the left, swung to the right — never mind the gun, he was a weapon all on his own, Perry thought, watching his progress through the crack in the door.

Nick disappeared out of Perry's line of vision.

Perry waited. His eyes fell on something he had missed as he watched Nick. A pair of feet stuck out from behind the kitchen counter. Someone lay on the kitchen floor.

A wave of dizziness hit him; he closed his eyes and leaned back against the wall.

Another body. They ought to change the name of this place to Homicide House.

When he opened his eyes and looked again, Nick was stealthily cutting from the hallway into the bedroom.

A moment later he stuck his head around the corner.

"Get in here, Foster. Someone knocked Stein out."

"*Stein?* How did he get up here so fast?"

"I don't know. I just know he's here and unconscious."

Stein was making an effort to sit up when Perry and Nick joined him on the kitchen linoleum.

"What the hell happened?" he muttered.

"Someone cold-cocked you," Nick replied. "Did you see who?"

Stein felt the top of his head. "Shit, what'd he hit me with? A baseball bat?"

A visible lump rose out of his iron gray part.

"Probably that," Perry said, pointing to the fireplace poker, which was wrapped in a paint-spattered rag.

"I guess I oughta be grateful he wasn't trying to kill me."

"He?" Nick questioned.

"He or she."

"What happened?"

"The door was open so I walked in."

"*Why?*" Perry asked.

Stein admitted, "I guess I just assumed it was you two. Anyway, I heard a movement behind me. He must have been behind the door. I turned and he slammed me over the head."

Nick asked, "But you didn't see who it was?"

Stein shook his head, then winced.

"The bedroom window was open," Nick said.

"He must have got out that way," Perry said, meeting his eyes. "Otherwise we'd have seen him going down the stairs."

Nick nodded slowly. "Unless he started downstairs before we left my place. He'd have to be moving pretty fast. See if you can locate the deputy. He's got to be here somewhere."

"Maybe he's disappeared, like Tiny," Stein mumbled.

Wide-eyed, Perry turned back to Nick, who shook his head. "Nah. No way. He's either inside Watson's apartment, or he's snooping around downstairs."

Perry jumped up and raced down the stairs. He reached the landing and was starting down the second flight when someone called, "Hey, Foster! Where's the fire?"

It was Deputy Abe back in his chair outside Watson's apartment door.

Perry skidded to a stop and stared down the long hall.

"Where were you?"

The deputy raised a coffee mug. "Downstairs. Getting something hot to drink. This place is like a morgue."

"Mr. Stein was knocked out upstairs in my apartment."

"Who? Stein? What was he doing in your apartment? Where were you?"

"I was staying with Nick. Mr. Reno."

"The *SEAL*?" The surprise in the deputy's voice was not flattering. Perry flushed. Not that there was anything to be embarrassed about — unfortunately.

He said shortly, "Mr. Stein heard footsteps. He went up to investigate."

"Why didn't he call me?"

"He couldn't find you."

The deputy looked uncomfortable. "Oh, yeah. I was...er...talking with Ms....um...Bridger."

Miss Scarlet in the kitchen, Perry thought grimly amused. He waited for the deputy to set aside his mug and then led the way back upstairs.

"A lot of screwy things happen in this house," the deputy commented.

"Tell me about it," Perry muttered.

They found Stein on his feet, though listing a bit, refusing offers of paramedics.

"An ice pack," he said. "Coupla aspirin. I'll be good as new."

"You could have a concussion," Nick said. "I'd get checked out if I were you."

"No, you wouldn't," Stein said caustically.

And Nick's cheek creased in a reluctant smile. "Maybe not," he agreed.

The deputy asked all the obvious questions while Stein grew more impatient and gray with each passing moment.

"How many ways can I say it?" he asked finally. "I didn't see a goddamned thing."

"I'm just trying to do my job," the deputy said, injured. "This is what they pay me for."

"Is that so? I'm not impressed with how my tax dollars are spent. When I was on the force..."

They all tuned out at that, Deputy Abe turning a jaundiced eye on the informal gallery of Perry's paintings. As Stein's reminiscences wound down, he asked, "Are these worth anything?"

Perry shrugged.

The deputy frowned at a painting of a field of berries ripening in the autumn sun. "I don't see the point of painting something like this when you can just take a photograph."

"It's not the same thing," Perry said.

"No, because a photograph is more accurate."

"Art isn't just about accuracy. It's about interpretation. It's about —"

Nick said, in the tone of one making a real effort, "I don't think an art critic broke in here."

The deputy shrugged as though personally unconvinced.

"This is the last time I do the neighborly bit," Stein grumbled. He was headed slowly for the front door. He gestured to Nick. "Next time I'll let you take point. You seem trained for it."

That reminded the deputy. "By the way, do you have a permit for that cannon?" He was eyeing Nick narrowly.

"Yep." Nick smiled tightly. "I'm the law-abiding type."

The deputy held his gaze, then turned to Perry. "Anything missing?"

"No."

"You haven't checked," Nick pointed out.

Perry gave him an ungrateful look and walked quickly down the hall to the bedroom.

The deputy said, "I guess I'll poke around a little. See what I turn up."

"You could check the bedroom window for fingerprints," Nick suggested.

"I'm glad you thought of that," the deputy drawled. "What would the sheriff's department do without you?"

Perry returned. "I don't think anything's missing. I can't tell that anyone was even in here."

"Come on," Nick said. "Let's leave it to the professionals. We don't want to make life harder for them than it already is."

§ § § §

"That's it," Perry said as they reached Nick's rooms, and the door slammed shut behind them. "I've had it. I can't stay here. I'll never feel safe here again." He began to pace, rubbing the palms of his hands nervously up and down his thighs.

"Whoa. What's this about?" Nick reached out and grabbed Perry's shoulder, bringing him to a stop.

Perry regarded him with those fawn-colored eyes. He looked scared and angry, and his voice shook as he said, "I don't know what it's about. That's the whole trouble. But there's something *wrong* here. Can't you feel it?"

Nick was feeling something all right — and it was most definitely wrong — but that didn't stop him from slowly drawing Perry toward him until their mouths were so close he could feel Perry's quick breaths against his lips.

Perry's mouth was pink and unsteady. He gazed up into Nick's eyes and then lowered his lashes, relaxing in Nick's hold.

He didn't make a move toward Nick, he just waited docilely for whatever was going to happen, to happen.

Christ, he was young. Nick tried to remember what it felt like to be that young — he didn't think he had ever been *that* young. Too young, too passive, too inexperienced.

A total twink. Cute, though.

Nick let Perry go, stepping back. He looked away so he didn't have to see the disappointment on the kid's face.

Perry sucked in a sharp breath and looked up. He didn't speak. The silence took on a strained quality.

"Look," Nick said briskly. "By the time I leave here, this will all be sorted out. There's only so many possibilities, you know?"

Perry had turned away and was facing the rain-speckled window. His shoulders were rigid. He said roughly, "Really? When are you leaving?"

"I've got a few loose ends to tie up. It'll be a couple of weeks." Nick was surprised to hear himself say this after telling Roscoe and the guys that there was nothing to keep him from pulling up stakes immediately.

But he couldn't walk out and leave Foster in this jam. No fucking way was he leaving him until this thing was past crisis point.

Perry sighed. His shoulders relaxed, and he turned to face Nick. "Well, personally, I think if it's going to get sorted out, we're the ones who'll have to do it. I was thinking maybe I would try the historical society today. See if I could find some more information on the history of the house."

This aggressive, hands-on approach took Nick aback and didn't quite jibe with his image of Perry Foster as a damsel in distress. Still, he was relieved beyond measure that the kid was taking his withdrawal calmly. He had been on guard against an emotional outburst. Foster's calm redirect to the problem at hand was unexpected — and welcome.

"What about getting hold of a copy of the blueprints?" Nick asked.

"There won't be blueprints for the original structure," Perry said. "Before 1900, builders didn't draw up elaborate plans like they do now. Not with the kind of specs architects provide these days. There might be some kind of plans from the renovations done when Alston bought the place in the twenties."

"Would Mrs. Mac have them?"

"Maybe. But do we want her to know we're looking that closely into the history of the house?"

Once again, Nick was nonplussed by this unexpected shrewdness on Foster's part.

"What are our other options?"

Foster considered. "We could try the building inspector's office at Town Hall. They must have filed for permits when they did the last bunch of renovations, when the house was gutted for apartments. That was probably done in the last twenty years or so. I'm not sure when Mrs. Mac took over."

"Does she own the place or does she manage it for someone else?"

"Now that you mention it, I don't know." Perry thought it over. "Everyone sort of assumes she owns the place. Maybe she doesn't. We should find out. And we could also check out the fire insurance maps while we're at Town Hall. Some of those date back to the late 1800s. You can get a good three-dimensional view sometimes. Something that would indicate the outlines of buildings, the placements of doors, windows, porches —"

"You're still thinking secret passage," Nick said. He wasn't jeering at the idea as he had before.

"I guess so, yeah. Somebody got upstairs past the deputy."

"The deputy could have been downstairs a lot longer than he's saying — or even realizes."

"True." But clearly Perry was only giving lip service to this idea, because he added, "We could try the city archives too, or maybe the library. Definitely the historical society. The house has always been one of the important ones in the area, even back when it was Hennesey Farm. I'm sure some version of the plans will be in historical records somewhere."

"You seem to know a lot about this stuff," Nick said curiously.

Perry's expression grew vague. He said, "I was studying to be an architect for a while. It wasn't my thing, though."

"Your thing is painting," Nick said, watching him.

"Yes." Perry changed the subject. "The other possibility is what they used to call pattern books. A lot of turn of the century builders got their ideas from stock plans published by different companies. But I don't think those would give us a clue to any secret passages or hidden tunnels. Those would probably be unique to the house."

"Okay," Nick said, reaching for his jacket. "Sounds like we've got a plan. Let's start with the historical society and work from there."

§ § § §

Jane was taking delivery of a pizza as they reached the front hall. She paid the girl in her brightly colored uniform and locked the door against the rain and wind, starting as she spied Nick and Perry.

"The breakfast of champions," Nick remarked, taking in the familiar logo on the flat pizza box.

"Hey, it's after noon," Jane said. "Besides, I like pizza for breakfast."

"You're not going to work again?" Perry asked.

"No." She lowered her voice. "I just heard about Mr. Stein getting clobbered in your apartment."

"He said he heard someone walking around in my rooms," Perry said.

"And he went upstairs to investigate? That was civic-minded of him."

Nick scrutinized her. "Why do you think he went upstairs?"

"I have no idea," Jane said. "Maybe he did hear someone walking around, but everyone in this place is starting to act very strange. I noticed Miss Dembecki wandering around in the garden a while ago, and I had to call to her four times before she came inside. I hope she's not losing it. I don't think she has any family." Jane resumed normal speaking tones. "So where are you two off to?"

"Town," Perry said succinctly.

"You might want to rethink that. There's another storm on the way." She shivered. "Mr. Teagle thinks the bridge will flood out for sure."

"Gee, wouldn't it be too bad if we couldn't get back," Perry said sarcastically.

"Oh, but it would!" Jane said. "You'll miss the séance."

Perry, who had one hand on the door handle, stopped. "What séance?"

"D — Mr. Center — has agreed to conduct a séance tonight here in the house."

"You gotta be kidding me," Nick said.

At the same moment, Perry demanded, "A séance? *Why?*"

Jane said defensively, "Why, because of the haunting, of course!" But she was avoiding his accusing gaze.

"That's ridiculous," Perry said with unusual heat. "A ghost never hit Stein over the head. No ghost shot Tiny."

"I never said a ghost hit Stein over the head. Not that I would blame them."

"Whose idea was this séance?" Perry demanded, his pale face flushing with angry color. "Who are you supposed to be contacting in the spirit world?"

Jane looked impatient. "Your ghost, of course."

Perry's mouth parted, and he seemed to struggle for air. Nick put an unobtrusive hand on his arm. The younger man was shaking. "He isn't mine! Anyway, he *wasn't* a ghost."

"David says it was."

"He wasn't there! I was."

Jane was now red as well. "Well, sweetie, sometimes it takes an expert to tell the difference."

Perry's mouth moved, but no words seemed forthcoming. He seemed genuinely at a loss — or maybe just inarticulate with anger.

"You're not going to win this argument," Nick told him, his hand tightening on the tensed arm. "Come on." He opened the door and thrust Perry outside.

"You'll be back in time for the séance, right?" Jane threw after them. "You've got to be here, Perry. David says we need your presence."

"Don't wait up for us," Nick told her and closed the door on her indignant face.

"Everyone in that fucking house has gone insane," Perry cried as they ran across the flooded scraggy lawn. "Why doesn't anybody see what's really going on here?"

They reached Nick's pickup. Nick unlocked the passenger door and ran around to his side. Perry was still fuming as Nick started the engine.

"Just cool down," Nick said, a little amused. "Nobody can make you do anything you don't want to."

Perry stared at him in open astonishment. "Do you really believe that?"

Nick considered. "I'm not talking about death and taxes, but yeah. Up to a point, yeah. Sure as hell no one can force you to attend some psychic tea party if you don't want to."

Perry made a small, bitter, and dismissive noise, turning his face to the steaming window.

"What's that supposed to mean?" Nick shot a quick, curious glance his way.

"Nothing." Nick looked his way again, as they bumped onto the long covered bridge, but Perry's expression was lost in the darkness of the tunnel. Nick could feel the buzz of his emotions like an electrical field.

"What's with you?"

"Nothing."

"What's wrong?"

Perry said quietly, "People have all kinds of ways of forcing you to do what you don't want to."

"I don't even know what we're talking about," Nick said. "I'm not going to let anyone force you to take part in some hocus-pocus bullshit. You can count on that."

Silence.

The truck exited the darkness of the covered bridge, and Nick risked another glance at his companion. Perry was still staring out the window, his expression oddly cold and removed.

§ § § § §

"Verity Lane," Mrs. Bartlett said with a reminiscent twinkle in her eyes. "I think they're showing one of her films down the street."

Perry wondered if the elderly Mrs. Bartlett, curator of the Fox Run Historical Society, just might — in the words of Jane — be losing it, but she relieved his mind by clarifying, "They're holding one of those vintage film revivals at the Players Theater on Dove Street. The matinee is just two dollars. They're calling it the 'two-bits matinee.'"

"We were more interested in Shane Moran," Nick said. He was examining the display of disabled eighteenth-century firearms.

"Oh, but you can't understand Shane without discussing Verity," Mrs. Bartlett said, amused. "They were lovers, you see."

"I thought she was married to Henry Alston," Perry objected with the naive surprise of the product of a stable, middle-class union.

"She was! It was a terrible scandal. Alston was a stuffy New Englander, but rich as Croesus when he bought the house at the start of Prohibition and set about renovating it. He had fallen in love with one of the Ziegfeld Girls, Verity Lane, and the story is he bought the old Hennesey Farm for her, although why he thought a little butterfly like Verity would want to live in the wilds of Vermont…"

To keep her to himself, Perry thought. But he didn't say anything, letting Mrs. Bartlett run on unchecked.

"The story goes that Verity originally spurned him — several times and quite publicly at that, but he persisted and eventually won her over. They moved here in 1923, and became quite famous for their wild parties. I shouldn't say *their*, because I supposed *that* was all Verity, with Henry simply hanging on for dear life."

"I read an article on the house," Perry said. "Hot jazz and hooch. And illegal gambling."

"And that's where Shane Moran comes in," Mrs. Bartlett said. "It was Prohibition, of course, and the sale, transport, and manufacture of alcohol were illegal in the United States."

"Hard to believe they got that passed," Nick said.

"The temperance movement has a long history in Vermont," Mrs. Bartlett said. "But you're quite right. The Eighteenth Amendment was extremely unpopular with the vast majority of people in this country, and that created an enormous market for contraband and served to legitimize the criminal element. Otherwise law-abiding citizens began to do business with gangsters such as Shane Moran. Because of its proximity to the Canadian border, Vermont was a corridor for bootleggers and rumrunners."

Mrs. Bartlett led them down an aisle, past a series of lithographs of early village life and household utensils to a montage of old photographs.

"This was Shane Moran."

Perry had been expecting someone who looked like Al Capone — or at least Humphrey Bogart — but Moran was a clean-cut-looking young man with rough-hewn Irish features. Perry studied the photo. One thing for sure: this was not a picture of the dead man in the bathtub.

Nick said, "So Henry Alston started buying booze for his big parties from Shane Moran and...what? He tried to double-cross Moran?"

"I see you have a cynical view of human nature," Mrs. Bartlett said. She was twinkling again, so apparently she approved of Nick's jaded worldview.

"I've been around," Nick replied.

"Apparently Henry *did* try to pull a fast one on Moran, but it might not have been entirely Henry's fault. The story I heard from my grandmother, who was a maid at the Alston Estate, was that Verity fell in love with Shane Moran."

"Uh-oh," Perry said.

"Henry's words exactly, I suppose," Mrs. Bartlett agreed. "Henry wanted Moran out of the picture, and so the story goes he tried to set up some kind of sting with immigration agents. Moran got away."

"And then Moran crashed Henry's private party and robbed him and his wealthy guests," Nick said. "I'm surprised Moran didn't just shoot Alston."

"Oh, Moran wasn't a killer. At least not a cold-blooded one. And in any case, what he really came for was Verity." Mrs. Bartlett pointed with one gnarled hand, the golden wedding glinting dully.

"I didn't read anything about *that*," Perry said.

"It didn't make it into the local papers, although it was quite well known in these parts. Moran showed up and begged Verity to come away with him, but I suppose the role of gangster's moll didn't appeal to her. Anyway, he left with a fortune in jewels and valuables — but without Verity. He was caught in the woods at Witch Hollow a few days later and gunned down by lawmen who, so the story goes, had been bribed by Henry Alston to make sure Moran was not brought in alive."

"And the fortune in jewels and valuables was never located?" Perry asked.

"Correct. There are all kinds of stories about that. But the most likely answer is that Moran's confederates took the loot away with them. Although as far as anyone knows, not so much as a pinky ring ever turned up."

"How would anyone know?" Perry asked. "Maybe the jewels were broken up and sold out of state."

"Verity was wearing the Alston sapphires. It was a very valuable and well-known collection. There was a necklace, two bracelets, and a ring. It would have been hard to fence any part of that without someone recognizing the stones — the robbery got a great deal of attention in the media. And several of the other guests lost quite valuable pieces in addition to the usual gold cigarette lighters and silver compacts." Mrs. Bartlett smiled her sweet, apple-cheeked smile. "I think word would have got out if any of that haul had turned up."

"Why didn't Moran leave?" Nick wondered aloud, frowning as he considered the long-dead gangster's photograph. "Why keep hanging around after the Lane broad turned him down?"

"Maybe he thought she'd change her mind," Perry said.

Nick gave him a level look. "Sounds like she made her feelings pretty clear."

"That's just another one of those things we'll never know," Mrs. Bartlett said, apparently untroubled at the idea.

"Who owns the house now?" Nick questioned.

"Now *that's* a very interesting question," Mrs. Bartlett said. "Of course, Mrs. MacQueen has managed the property — if you can call it that — for nearly twenty years, but the house has changed hands many times since Alston lost his fortune in March of '33. It's currently owned by the Dunstan family in Barre. In fact, one of the current tenants is a distant relation."

"Who?" Perry asked.

"Jim Teagle," answered Mrs. Bartlett.

CHAPTER NINE

"It's not exactly an amazing coincidence," Nick said, raising a bottle of Sam Adams to his mouth. "What you've got is somebody farming out their pain-in-the-ass elderly relative to live for free or nearly for free in one of their investment properties. Teagle can keep an unofficial eye on the place — and Mrs. MacQueen — and it relieves the relatives from having to deal with him. We haven't heard anything to indicate there's a connection with the Alstons or with Shane Moran." He drank from the bottle.

"It's funny he never mentioned it," Perry said, raising his voice to be heard over the large-screen plasma TV in one corner, where two college football teams were charging into each other.

"Do you tell him everything?" Nick inquired. "Did you tell him your reason for going to San Francisco?"

"Well, no," Perry admitted.

They were grabbing a bite at the Moosehead Tavern on Bank Street. Leather-lined booths, a pool table in the adjacent room, and the head of a moose wearing a Santa Claus hat mounted over the bar — it was not Perry's kind of hangout, but he felt comfortable with Nick sitting across the table. Nick sipped his beer, his dark blue eyes flicking to the TV screen now and then.

"What's the job?" Perry asked.

"Hmm?" Nick's eyes met his.

"In Los Angeles. Your new job."

"Oh." To Perry's surprise, Nick's color deepened. "Private investigator."

Perry's face lit up with interest. "For real?"

"Yeah." Nick sounded sheepish. "A SEAL buddy of mine started up the firm with some friends of his." He shrugged.

"You'll be great at that," Perry said.

That seemed to make Nick more uncomfortable. He said, "It's nothing like the movies — or those books you read. It's a lot of background and vehicle locates."

Perry suggested hopefully, "Insurance fraud? Missing persons?"

"Yeah, maybe," Nick admitted. "It's still not like the movies."

"How do you know?"

"I *hope* it's not like the movies," Nick said, and Perry chuckled.

The waitress came over to their table, and they ordered food and a couple more beers. She returned shortly with chicken cheesesteak for Perry and smoked pork chili topped with Vermont cheddar and onions for Nick. Nick was thinking that this was one of the things he was going to miss in California: the chili and the honey and jalapeño cornbread.

He glanced up, and Perry was smiling at him. That was another thing he was going to miss in California, but it was better not to think about that. Instead, he said, "Listen, I've been doing some thinking."

Perry got that inquiring look — as though Nick's thoughts were always worth his full attention.

Nick said, "Did anyone know you had changed your plans for the weekend? Did anyone know you were coming back early?"

"No."

"Why *did* you come back early?"

Perry stared at him. "I told you. It didn't work out with my friend."

"Okay, what about this friend of yours? Where did you meet him?"

"Over the Internet."

"Over the *Internet*? You mean, like in a chat room?"

"Yes." Perry's chin got an unexpectedly mulish jut to it. "So what? Lots of people meet that way. We started e-mailing each other, and it turned out we had a lot in common. Marcel was --"

Nick put his beer down. "*Marcel?*"

"Marcel, yes," Perry said shortly.

"You were having a cyber-romance with someone named *Marcel?*" Nick was laughing at him, and Perry turned red with anger.

"You make it sound stupid and weird. It wasn't. We had a real friendship. A real relationship. We wrote each other every day, sometimes a couple of times a day. So then we finally called each other on the phone. We talked a long time, and we decided to meet, to see —"

"And surprise, surprise," Nick said cynically. "He was three feet tall, bald, fat, and pushing sixty."

Perry said hotly, "He was *exactly* like I expected. Like I hoped. He was *perfect.*"

Nick's mouth curved sardonically, but all he said was, "So what happened with Mr. AOL? You weren't what *he* expected?"

Perry stared at him, stricken. He said at last, "His ex-boyfriend wanted to get back together."

Even Nick blinked at that one. "Jesus. He couldn't have picked a different weekend?"

Perry's anger was already spent. He smiled lopsidedly. "I guess it would have been nice if they'd figured it out before I spent all that money on plane tickets and three new shirts. It took forever to save up."

"So now you're short rent money because you wasted it on new clothes and a trip."

Perry nodded.

Nick studied him critically but not unkindly. "Didn't it occur to you…?"

"You don't understand," Perry said. "I thought I knew him. I *do* know him. He's…he's smart and funny and sensitive. He's an architect. Someday he's going to build something as amazing as…as Frank Lloyd Wright. We had a *lot* in common. We had the same favorite movie in high school — *Come Undone* — and we have the same favorite song — "Human" by the Killers. We both like our corn on the cob barbecued, and cinnamon and nutmeg in our cocoa. And neither of us watched *Queer as Folk*, *and* we both had golden retrievers when we were kids."

Strictly speaking, it was more than he and Marie had ever had in common. Nick said, "He didn't mention the ex-boyfriend to you?"

The prosaic question brought Perry up short. "Sort of. I knew he'd been in a relationship. Who hasn't?"

"Have you?"

"I haven't *lived* with anyone," Perry said with great dignity.

Nick shook his head.

"It's not that easy to meet people here," Perry told him. "Vermont isn't all…I mean, parts of it are conservative. Especially in the Kingdom. This is a small town."

"So move."

"Where?" Even in the murky light, Nick could see the delicate wash of color beneath Foster's clear skin. "It takes money. First and last month's rent, and I don't even have this month's rent. And I'd have to find a new job. I'm not really trained for anything."

Nick considered him. "I can't help you there, but I'll tell you what. My rent's paid for the next two months. I paid six months in advance. When I go, you can stay on here. That should get you time to catch up."

Perry gazed at him, speechless.

"Don't make a big deal of it," Nick warned.

"No. Right." Perry lowered his lashes. He seemed to be struggling to repress a smile as he devoted himself to his French fries.

"Okay, that's settled," Nick said briskly. "Now all we have to do is figure out who dumped that body in your bathtub." He wasn't entirely serious. At least…he thought they might uncover information that might help the sheriff's department with their lame-ass investigation, and he thought it was good to keep the kid's mind occupied. But Nick really didn't have hopes they would crack the case of the disappearing corpse.

"Whoever killed Tiny," Perry replied — apparently under the illusion that they were really going to bust this thing wide open.

"Maybe."

"That had to be it. Tiny was going around blabbing about seeing the ghost with yellow socks, and that must have posed some kind of danger for someone."

Nick said, "But you realize he was talking about that to us while we were in Watson's apartment."

Those ridiculous lashes swept up. "You mean someone was listening to us."

This was one of the things Nick did like about Foster. He could put two and two together without a song and dance.

"Yeah. I have trouble believing in secret passages, but I think either someone overheard Tiny talking to you, or Tiny mentioned 'the ghost' to one too many people."

"Center and Stein are both on that floor. Center's apartment is right next to Watson's — and they say blind people compensate with their other senses. Maybe he's got really acute hearing."

"Huh," Nick said.

They ate in silence while music played in the background. Christmas music. It was only November, but Bing Crosby was already hitting the airwaves. Nick found it vaguely depressing.

"We could try the library archives next," Perry said.

Nick nodded. He wasn't thrilled at the idea of spending the day in the library, but it wasn't like he had a lot of other ideas. This was about as cold a case as they came, so the obvious avenues of investigation were eliminated. Too bad this hadn't come up a few months after he had some P.I. training under his belt.

Of course, in a few months he would be in California, and Perry Foster would be just another memory of a time in his life he couldn't wait to put behind him.

"*Or,*" Perry suggested suddenly, hopefully, "We could go see the Verity Lane film at the Players Theater."

"That sounds like a waste of time."

"We don't have a lot of leads," Perry pointed out. "It couldn't hurt to see one of the principals, right?"

Oddly, Nick discovered that he didn't want to disappoint the kid — not that he could see any practical purpose in watching an old movie. Although he was mildly curious about Verity Lane.

"Maybe we could go to the library and then go see the film?"

When Nick didn't respond, Perry said very casually, "If you're worried about people thinking you're gay if you go with me, you don't have to be."

Nick met Perry's eyes levelly. "No?"

"No."

"Why's that?"

"You're not the type."

"There's a type, huh? I thought that was a myth. What about those queer bodybuilders?"

Perry shrugged. "I've never met one."

"You know a lot of bodybuilders?"

"No, but I know other gay guys. You know, I haven't lived my entire life here in Fox Run."

"I figured. Where are you from?"

"Rutland."

Second largest city in Vermont and a commercial hub, so Foster should have been relatively worldly. But Nick thought he had the picture. A sickly, overprotected little kid — he was betting on only child of doting older parents.

"What are you doing here in the boondocks?"

"I thought it would be fun to live in a small town." The cheerful cluelessness of that almost took Nick's breath away. "You know, someplace where everyone knows your name, and you don't have to lock your car or your doors. And I thought it would be good for my painting to live someplace rural and quiet."

"It didn't occur to you it might get a little lonely for someone with your orientation?"

Perry was silent. "I wasn't thinking about that so much. I wanted to get away."

"From what?"

"Everything. Everyone I knew. Everything I knew."

Nick said mildly, "Sounds a little drastic."

Perry stared out the pub window at the Thomas Kincaid streets glistening in the rain. The colored blur of shop lights, streetlights, car lights reflected in the wet blacktop. Nick hoped he wasn't going to confide his life story.

Perry said matter-of-factly, "When I told my parents I was gay, they threw me out."

The background noise of the TV swelled and dipped. Nick sipped his beer, set the mug down with careful deliberation. "Why'd you tell them?"

Perry looked confused. "They're my parents."

"Exactly. You must have known them well enough to know how they felt on the subject."

"But I thought — it should — make a difference that it was *me*."

"You thought that they would feel different about something that shocked and disgusted them if their darling little boy told them he was one of *them*? You really are naive."

Perry reddened. "They love me. I love them. I *had* to be honest."

This idea was alien to Nick. He had enlisted in the navy when he was eighteen — five years younger than Foster was now. He would no more have discussed his sexual inclinations with his parents than he would have eaten the family dog. True, his mom and dad had been busy providing for six kids and his grandmother. Heartfelt confidences hadn't been a big part of the Reno family life. Discussion in general hadn't been something his folks had a lot of time or energy for. It had been all they could do to keep food on the table and clothes on their backs.

Besides, Nick had married Marie right before he went into the service — mostly because that's what people did in Island Pond. It had never occurred to him to do anything else — not for a very long time.

Funny. Depending on how you looked at it, Foster was miles ahead of where Nick had been at that age.

Perry said staunchly, "They'll come around when they realize…"

"It's not a phase?"

He nodded.

"Are you sure it's not?"

Perry's eyes darkened. "Of course, I'm sure."

"I mean, you've never been with anybody, right?" Nick was blunt. "Male or female? It's my experience that a lot of young guys are scared of girls."

To his surprise, Perry relaxed, chuckling, "I'm not scared of girls. My best friends have always been girls. Guys never had time for me in high school — except the other misfits."

Nick eyed him irritably.

"Girls don't interest me," Perry explained, as though spelling out the facts of life. "Guys like you interest me."

Nick dropped his cornbread.

"Anyway," Perry said off-handedly. "My parents threw me out, and there went my degree in architecture, which was okay. I wanted art school anyway. So I decided to go for it. Go after my dream and become a painter." He smiled cheerfully at Nick. "Of course, it really doesn't pay very well."

Nick felt like he had a headache coming on. It was his own fault. He'd just had to open his big mouth and ask, hadn't he?

§ § § §

The rain was turning to sleet as they parked in the library parking lot. Perry wrapped his scarf around his mouth and nose, but he was coughing as they got to the top of the stairs leading into the brick building.

"Don't you take some kind of regular medication to control that?" Nick asked, frowning as Perry struggled to catch his breath.

Perry shook his head. "I used to, but I don't have health insurance now."

"Christ Almighty."

Nick was staring at him in exasperation. "It's not bad in the summer. Or even the spring, really. It's just when it gets really cold that I sometimes have trouble," Perry assured him.

"No problem, then. Except you happen to live in Vermont."

Perry shrugged this off. His breathing was already steadying again. He turned and led the way into the quiet building.

"Can't stay away from the place, can you?" A plump, dark-haired girl greeted Perry from behind the reference desk. Then she noticed that Nick was actually with him and not just waiting in line. Her gaze grew curious. "Why, *hello.*"

"Hi."

"We're just going to look through the archives," Perry said, vaguely irritated by Patti's instant interest in Nick. Nick didn't even seem to notice it — maybe he was used to being a chick magnet. Maybe his thoughts were on other things — he wore that dark and brooding look again as he stared around at the brightly lit room, the construction paper decorations, the flyers of local events.

Patti said, "Not much of a vacation, is it?"

Perry smiled politely, but he was thinking that since Nick had shown up, his vacation had improved immeasurably.

The next three hours they spent poring over books and plastic-bound copies of the old *Gazettes*. Whether it was of any use was hard to say; it was clear that Nick did not think a lot of this kind of investigative work. He'd have preferred to be out pounding the pavement — and maybe a few heads. Every so often he would push back his chair and go stand at the window framed by little Christmas lights, staring out at the gloomy, wet afternoon.

It wasn't hard to picture Nick in a fedora facing down a pack of hired goons. He had the kind of face that would have looked perfect on a '40s pulp fiction cover.

"What are you looking at?" Nick asked suddenly, jarring Perry out of his reflections. He hadn't noticed he was staring, and he colored.

Nick's hard gaze continued to hold his — a strange moment passed — then Nick glanced back out the window and said, "Anything interesting in those papers?"

"Well, one thing," Perry said slowly, still reading. "The Underground Railroad operated in these parts, and Oswald Hennesey was a fervent abolitionist."

"Oswald being a descendent of the Hennesey Farm Henneseys?"

Perry nodded. "Did you ever read a book called *The House of Dies Drear?*"

"Doesn't ring a bell."

"I read it in junior high. It's about this kid who moves into a house that was used in the Underground Railroad. Everybody thinks the house is haunted by the ghost of an abolitionist named Dies Drear, but it turns out that the family next door is trying to scare people away so they can steal the treasure buried beneath the tunnels."

"Oh boy," Nick said. "I see where this is heading."

"I'm just sayin'…" Perry was grinning as he returned to his reading.

However he didn't find anything indicating that Hennesey Farm was actually part of the Underground Railroad let alone that it contained secret passages, and it turned out that Oswald Hennesey had not even lived on the estate. After that brief excitement, Perry's reading was pretty boring until he found a couple of 1920s newspaper clippings about Henry Alston buying Hennesey Farm.

"Here's a picture of Verity Lane," he said, offering one of the books to Nick.

Nick studied the smudged and faded photos. Lane had been a flat-chested, platinum blonde with a bow mouth and wide eyes. Vaguely reminiscent of a Jean Harlow, Lane had been beautiful in the way of women of her era.

Perry was still reading through the clippings. "This file is almost all about the Alstons." The papers had apparently routinely regaled Depression-era readers with reports of wild parties at the Alston Estate attended by the celebrities and VIPs of the day. Unsurprisingly, the Shane Moran robbery had made the headlines.

"Here's some stuff on the party itself."

Nick set aside the pictures of Verity Lane and looked over Perry's shoulder.

Perry read, "It was a gala event. Chinese lanterns decorated the terrace. The guests dined on roasted squab and danced to the music of Ted Olsen's Orchestra. Just before midnight, gangster Shane Moran burst in with his gang, robbing the gentlemen and relieving the ladies of their jewels. The famed Alston sapphires, including a necklace valued at over twenty thousand dollars, were snatched from the mistress of the house.

"I wonder what that necklace would be worth now," Perry interrupted himself to add.

"Plenty," Nick answered.

Subsequent articles dealt with the police hunt for the gangsters. Two of the men were eventually captured at a speakeasy in Sugarbrush, but the others had disappeared. Moran, of course, had only eluded capture for a couple of days before being cornered in the woods surrounding the estate. The official story was that he had refused the chance to surrender peaceably and had been shot to death by local law enforcement.

There was no explanation — oddly enough, there was not even speculation — as to why Moran had tried to return to the scene of the crime. No trace had ever been found of the jewels and other valuables taken on that long ago midsummer evening.

Thoughtfully, Perry closed the binder.

"What?" Nick inquired, studying his face.

"There couldn't be anyone still left from that fateful party, could there? If someone had been twenty then, they would be in their nineties now, wouldn't they?"

"Pretty old to be pulling pranks at the old homestead," Nick agreed, seeing where this was going.

"Nobody at the estate is that old. Mr. Teagle is in his seventies, and Miss Dembecki must be around there. Mrs. Mac is probably..." Perry squinted, trying to place Mrs. Mac.

"Sixties," Nick said with certainty. "Stein's probably a little younger. Not a lot."

It was clear to Perry that Nick was getting restless.

They finished poring over the records of houses in the area, and Perry found a map that he showed Nick.

They bent over it, heads close together, and out of the corner of his eyes he could see the blue shadow beneath Nick's smoothly shaven cheek, the flicker of his eyelashes, the strong, uncompromising chin and blunt nose.

Nick's eyes flicked his way as though feeling Perry's attention, and then returned to the map.

"Doesn't look like the basic structure changed externally. They mostly added walls inside, making more rooms."

They finished at the library and walked out on the street. It was about four o'clock and already getting dark. Nick glanced at his watch, then at Perry who — red plaid scarf wrapped protectively over his mouth and nose — was gazing at him hopefully.

"You want to go see that damn matinee, don't you?" he said, resigned.

"Unless you have plans," Perry said politely through the folds of worsted.

Nick sighed.

They found Nick's truck and drove over to Dove Street, Perry gazing silently out the window at the houses decorated for Christmas. Wire-framed lighted reindeer pretended to nibble sparse, brown lawns. Colored icicles dangled from eaves, and air-blown Santas bravely bobbed beneath the sleet and rain.

Perry had never felt less enthused about the holiday. Last year he had been full of hopes for the future. He had just moved into his airy tower at the Alston estate and was enjoying having his own place at last. His unease hadn't begun until later. He'd found the job in the library, the painting was going well, and he'd just met Marcel online. He had dreamed that perhaps by the same time the following year, he and Marcel might…well, no use thinking that way now.

SAINTS AND SINNERS STARRING JACK OAKIE AND VERITY LANE read the lit marquee atop the Players Theater.

Nick parked in the mostly deserted parking lot in the back and said, "Don't ever say I never did anything for you."

"I would never say that," Perry returned quite seriously, pulling his scarf up again.

They walked inside the old movie house; Nick bought a giant tub of popcorn with the air of a man drowning his sorrows in butter topping, and they found seats in the empty theater.

The film was already about five minutes in, but it didn't matter. As far as Perry could make out, it was something to do with an heiress running away to be with her horse trainer boyfriend. The horse trainer turned out to be no good, but the owner of the stable was one of those square-jawed good guys — and he was approved by the heiress's parents — so it looked like everything was going to work out.

Nick offered his tub of popcorn at frequent intervals, and every so often their hands brushed diving into the carton of hot kernels.

Verity Lane was small and blonde and animated. To Perry she looked like all those other small, blonde, pert actresses of her day. He did not get a particular sense of her personality — she seemed like a squeaky-voiced anachronism, a little platinum ghost come to life for a few hours.

What about her had inspired Shane Moran to risk death? It was a mystery to Perry. Maybe Nick had a different opinion. He glanced over. Nick watched without expression; Perry could see the shadows from the projector play across his face.

He tried to picture Nick married to someone, but the picture just wouldn't form.

His thoughts wandered as Verity Lane flirted and wisecracked and wept through the remaining twenty minutes of film. *What had happened to Verity after Shane Moran was killed?* wondered Perry. *Had she and Henry Alston remained together?* Henry had lost his fortune a year of so after Moran was shot to death. Had Verity gone back to making movies? He didn't remember her as one of those aging movie queens on late-night TV. He had the vague notion she'd quit making movies. He couldn't recall seeing her in anything as she was older; she had made the transition to talkies, but then what?

"*Say,*" Verity sassed in the arms of a dime-a-dozen matinee idol, having the last line before the fade to black. "Just what kind of a gal do you think I *am?*"

Nick snorted. He turned to Perry. In the darkness Perry could only see the gleam of eyes and what might have been a resigned grin. "Happy now?" Nick asked softly, and there was a note in his voice…indulgent?

And with an uneasy flash, Perry realized he *was* happy. Happy because Nick was with him. It wiped the smile off his own face. In a week or two Nick would be gone — they would probably never see each other again. Getting attached to Nick would be even stupider than getting attached to Marcel had been.

It was dark when they walked out of the theater.

Perry was thinking how much he didn't want to head back to the Alston mansion, when Nick said casually, "Let's grab a beer."

They crossed the street to a disreputable-looking bar with a neon sign offering a half-tilted cocktail glass. Inside the bar was dark and smoky — although no one had legally smoked there for several years — and a jukebox was playing the Young Dubliners. A couple of hard young men in flannel shirts hunched over the bar talking to the bartender.

It was the kind of place Perry would not have dreamed of setting foot in on his own, but with Nick beside him, it held all the fascination of a quick trip to a foreign land.

Nick nodded toward a table, and Perry sat down while Nick went to the bar and ordered two beers. Perry watched Nick chatting and smiling with the men at the bar — he was obviously no stranger to the place.

"You want anything to eat?" Nick asked, setting the beer in front of Perry.

"They have food here?" Perry said, surprised.

Nick nodded.

Perry hesitated. "Are you having something?"

Nick read the hesitation correctly. And ordinarily he would have figured it was the kid's problem he didn't know how to budget, but…he was feeling flush. He had the Los Angeles job, and Roscoe had even offered an advance on his first paycheck. And…he liked to see Foster eat. He said brusquely, "Yeah. Why don't we get the potato skins? We can share. My treat."

He was rewarded with that shy smile.

"I guess it was kind of a waste of a day," Perry said later as they ate potato skins stuffed with golden cheddar cheese and bacon and sour cream. Nick had ordered a couple more beers by then, and under the influence of alcohol the kid had relaxed and grown chatty and confidential.

Nick shrugged.

"Do you think the sheriff will let us know what they learn?"

"You're assuming they'll learn anything," Nick said grimly, and Perry laughed. He was laughing a lot. Nick decided he didn't mind.

A new song came on the jukebox. A slow, romantic ballad, and Perry said suddenly, "Why didn't your marriage work out?"

Nick's face closed.

"Sorry," Perry said quickly. "I just…"

Nick said abruptly, "It didn't work out for the same reason a lot of marriages don't work out. By the end of it, we were completely different people than when we started. We didn't have anything in common."

Perry nodded. "Did you have anything in common when you started?"

It seemed an obvious question, but Nick stared at him. Then he gave a funny laugh. "Yeah, we came from the same town. I don't think it occurred to me we might need more. My parents were together for fifty-five years — till my old man died."

"My parents are still together," Perry offered.

"You an only kid?" Nick asked.

Perry nodded, and Nick nodded too as though this confirmed his thoughts.

They ate for a time in silence. Then Nick said, "I've been thinking about this séance."

Perry's mouth twisted, but he said, "I bet I know what you're going to say."

"Oh, you do?"

"You're going to say it would be useful to watch everyone who takes part in it, and that I should agree to attend."

"I do think it would be useful, yeah," Nick said. "I'm wondering if there's something else behind it — something besides Center being a wacko, I mean."

"What do you mean?"

"If I knew, I wouldn't drag you along with me."

Perry smiled, seemingly unperturbed at the idea of being dragged along by Nick. He was staring with those long-lashed eyes as though Nick was the most fascinating person on earth. *Flirting*, Nick thought amusedly. Maybe Perry didn't realize it himself.

He said, "You mean you think someone is going to try and ask Shane Moran what he did with the Alston sapphires?"

Nick shrugged. "Nothing would surprise me in that place. I wonder who exactly suggested that séance?"

Perry said slowly, "I got the feeling Jane did. I think she really likes Center. She might be pushing the idea of a séance as a way to get close to him. I never noticed her having any interest in ghosts and the supernatural before this."

"I suppose there's no doubt about how Watson died?" Nick asked.

Perry shook his head. "He had a heart attack in the village. It sounds pretty straightforward to me."

"It sounds like the fastest case of cause and effect on record," Nick remarked — which seemed a little harsh, given his own dietary habits. Perry covered a smile with his beer mug.

They finished their meal companionably, and Nick waved good night to the guys at the bar.

The drinks hit Perry going out to the car. He stumbled a little and said, "Man, I'm tired. I feel like I haven't slept in a week."

Nick took him by the arm and steered him to the pickup. "I think you'll sleep tonight."

Perry blinked up at and said seriously, "Couldn't we just stay in town tonight? Get a hotel room?"

"Are you making a move on me?" Nick asked amused.

Perry chuckled. "Want to experiment?" He smiled up at Nick trustingly.

Against his will, Nick laughed. "Not tonight, Josephine. We've got a séance to go to, remember?"

Perry made a face, though it was unclear whether at being turned down or at the recollection they were due to commune with the Great Beyond.

Nick unlocked the passenger door and went around to the driver's side. He started the engine.

Pulling out of the parking lot, he glanced Perry's way. He was so silent Nick thought he might have fallen asleep, but he was sitting up straight, staring expressionlessly out the window.

"You okay?"

He nodded.

"Listen," Nick said. "Nothing is going to happen to you while I'm around, so relax."

Perry said calmly, "I know. I'm just thinking about after you're gone."

CHAPTER TEN

The water was high and murky as they crossed the bridge. The lights of the Alston House shone with illusory warmth through the trees. The rains of the last couple of days had left the trees skeletal and stark white in the headlights of Nick's truck. Piles of tattered leaves scattered the wet earth.

They parked and walked around to the front. They were walking side by side, and perhaps Nick thought that Perry was still a little unsteady — he rested his hand lightly on the small of Perry's back.

"No police cars," Perry pointed out, taking pains not to show that he noticed Nick's hand resting above his ass.

Sure enough the yard was clear of any marked cars. Within, the house lights blazed on the lower level. More lights than Perry could ever remember seeing on at any one time in the old mansion.

Nick said, "Looks like they're planning a party."

Perry laughed nervously as he pushed open the front door.

The chandelier rocked musically in the winter's blast. Jane, wearing a black caftan, came to greet them. "There you are! We thought you'd never get here." She began to usher them toward the little-used "rec room."

Perry said, "Jeez, Janie, can we have a minute to take our jackets off?"

"You can take your jackets off in there. Everyone's been waiting."

"Who's everyone?" Nick inquired. He had removed his hand from Perry's back as they climbed the front steps, but he still stood close enough that their shoulders brushed. Perry couldn't decide if it was an accident or if Nick thought he needed reassurance.

"Everyone," Jane answered. Adding honestly, "I mean, what else is there to do on a night like this?"

"What happened to the cops?"

She made a face. "There's a big accident near the border. I guess they needed everyone there. It's not like there's much happening here."

"Just murder," said Perry.

Astonishingly, Jane said, "Tiny could have been shot by hunters. He could have dragged himself here."

"You're not serious," Perry said.

She shrugged, not meeting his eyes.

The lights had been turned down low as they walked into the room that served as the residence's meeting and recreation room — once the formal drawing room. There were bookshelves filled with used paperbacks, an old television set that never seemed to work, a heavy oval dining table that was supposed to be used for "games." Two large candelabra sat in the center of the table, casting uncertain light across the bleached wallpaper.

There were three empty chairs at the table. Mr. Teagle, Miss Dembecki, and Mrs. MacQueen were all in attendance. David Center sat at the table head, face turned attentively toward the door.

As Jane escorted Nick and Perry into the room, Center announced, "The spirits are eager to make contact tonight."

"Wonderful! You sit next to me, Perry," Jane instructed.

Perry's jaw got that hard look that sat so oddly with his Christopher Robin face. Nick said calmly, "Perry's good next to me."

Perry shot him a grateful look.

"Well!" Jane said, her smile a little forced as she looked from one to the other.

Perry and Nick took the two chairs at the table. There was an awkward silence.

Mr. Teagle said, "How's that river looking, son?"

"I don't think it will flood," Perry said. Mrs. Mac sat directly across from him. She was staring at him. He offered a polite smile. She licked her lips and looked away, reminding him forcibly of one of her unpleasant little dogs.

"If everyone would join hands," David Center instructed. "Left hand palm up to receive. Right hand palm down to transmit."

Calling the Twilight Zone.

Perry clasped hands with Miss Dembecki to his left and Nick to his right. Miss Dembecki's little hand was ice cold — as cold as his own, Perry thought. Nick's hand was warm. He squeezed Perry's with hard, quick reassurance, and as much as Perry did not want to be there, he felt a flare of happiness.

Center said, "For those of you who have not previously attended a séance, I should explain one or two things. There is nothing frightening or mysterious about communing with the dead. Spirits are around us all the time. They are part of the natural world, and if we open our hearts and minds, they are often willing to communicate."

Belatedly, Perry noticed that Rudy Stein was not at the table. It was hard to picture Stein taking part in a séance, but then, it was hard to picture himself taking part.

He sighed, and out of the corner of his eye saw Nick's mouth twitch.

Center said, "And this is all a séance amounts to: Communication between the physical world and the spirit world. This communication is moderated by one who is known as a medium. Tonight I will act as the medium as we attempt to call upon the spirits who still linger in this house."

Jane was smiling — beaming — at Center. He continued to talk seriously about the many séances he had conducted and how they all were ordinary, run-of-the-mill, and perfectly harmless. All in a day's work. If your day job was on the astral plane.

Perry said, "How are we going to contact the spirit of the man in my bathtub, when we don't even know his name?"

"Perry! Don't interrupt," Jane said.

Nick said, "Maybe we can just describe what he was last seen wearing." His eyes slanted to meet Perry's.

Perry relaxed, biting his lip.

"I understand nervousness can result in levity," Center said, "but the spirits don't like to be mocked. Now if I can ask everyone to remain silent while opening your hearts and minds…"

No one said anything. Perry closed his eyes. He could feel Miss Dembecki breathing quickly beside him. Her hand was still cold, and she was shaking very slightly. Granted, it *was* cold in the room. The house was always like an icebox. On the other hand — literally — he could feel the warmth and solid presence of Nick Reno.

He opened his eyes. Nick glanced at him. Grimaced. Everyone else at the table had their eyes closed, faces screwed up in concentration. Perry bit his lip against inappropriate laughter. But Center was right, he *was* nervous.

"Perry," Center said suddenly. Perry started. "Try to visualize the man you saw. Try to remember what his face looked like."

Perry closed his eyes and then opened them. He'd be just as happy not remembering that gray-green face, the white slits of eyes beneath half-closed lids… Impossible to think what the man would have looked like in life. It was much easier to remember the weave of that ugly plaid coat and those garish yellow socks.

It was very quiet in the room.

Perry's mind began to wander. He couldn't help it. He didn't believe in ghosts, and even if there was such a thing as a ghost, he sure as heck didn't want to attract its attention.

"Are you there?" Center asked softly, and for a moment Perry thought Center was talking to him. "Are you there? Do you wish to speak to someone here?"

No one said anything, but the silence took on a living, tense quality.

"I feel a presence," Center said all at once.

Perry studied the circle of faces. Mr. Teagle looked very pale, his face perspiring in the candlelight. Jane's face was taut with concentration. Mrs. Mac's eyes opened. She stared at Perry without expression, then closed her eyes like the Sphinx settling down for the night.

Center said in that low, hypnotic voice, "Why have you come here? What is it you wish to tell us? Who is it you wish to speak to?"

And then as though in answer to himself, Center said in a high, thin, eerily feminine voice, "Shane! Where are you? Why —"

"*There's someone in the mirror*," Miss Dembecki cried in terror. Eyes flew open, heads jerked, everyone turned to the mirror hanging over the fireplace.

For an instant, deceived by the shadows thrown by the candlelight, Perry thought that he too saw the reflection of someone framed in the mirror. The figure was indistinct, mutable...

The frozen hand clutching his suddenly relaxed, and Miss Dembecki slid to the floor in a dead faint.

§ § § §

"Shane! Come back, Shane!" Nick mocked in falsetto.

Perry managed a weak grin and took the mug of cocoa Nick offered.

They were back in Nick's apartment following the abrupt and dramatic end of the séance. Miss Dembecki had come around from her faint within a few seconds, but she had followed that with a bout of hysterical crying. It had been left to Jane and Mrs. Mac to calm her down and put her to bed.

"It did kind of look like someone was standing in the mirror," Perry said as Nick dropped down beside him onto the sofa.

"A woman," Nick agreed. "I saw it too. It was the reflection of the portrait on the opposite wall."

Perry's jaw dropped, and then he laughed. "I'm such a tool."

"Nah. You're just more imaginative and open-minded than I am."

Perry sipped his cocoa. It was piping hot. No marshmallows, but he thought he detected a hint of cinnamon and there was definitely a slug of something alcoholic. Whisky? Brandy? He said, "You have to admit it was kind of freaky the way Center changed his voice. He really did sound like a woman."

Nick shrugged. "It's one of the tricks of his trade, being able to throw his voice, change it."

"You don't think —"

"No, I don't," Nick answered.

Perry nodded. "I knew it would be a total waste of time." He took another sip of cocoa.

"I don't know," Nick said thoughtfully. "I'm wondering what Stein was doing while we were all gathered in the drawing room with John Edward."

"What do you think he was doing?"

Nick shook his head.

"I don't know what any of us were doing there, really," Perry said. "Except Janie. She's got something going on with Center, that's obvious."

"Yeah, she seems pretty taken with the guy," Nick agreed. "And Center... I wouldn't swear to it, but I think he believes his own bullshit."

"Miss Dembecki sure believes it," Perry said. "She wasn't faking. She was scared to death. That was a dead faint."

Miss Dembecki had been rag doll, limp and white. There was no faking that.

"Yep, and that's interesting too," Nick said. "Especially with what you were telling me about her poking around in the gazebo. How long has she lived here?"

"Years, I think. She and Mr. Teagle and Mrs. Mac have been here the longest."

Perry drained the rest of his cocoa, and Nick said, "You take the bed tonight, junior. You need to get some real rest."

"You know, I'm not actually twelve years old, Nick," Perry said.

"Hey, if you were twelve years old, I'd make you sleep on the couch," Nick said. "So enjoy the bed tonight."

Perry studied him with unusual gravity, then he collected his things and went to wash up. When he climbed into Nick's bed, the sheets and pillowcase smelled like Nick. He closed his eyes and let the sound of the rain sweep him into a comfortable blankness.

§ § § §

Nick waited till he heard the soft, even sound of Perry's breathing. Easing shut the bedroom door, he got his pistol and slipped out into the hallway.

There was no sign of anyone. The draperies puffed and flattened in the drafts, the dead plants stirring in the breeze.

Nick went quietly down the staircase; the house could have been empty.

On the second floor, he listened. Then he moved quietly. Pausing outside Center's door, he heard only dead silence. Even odds that Center was downstairs in Jane Bridger's apartment.

There was no light and no sound from Stein's apartment.

The door to Watson's room was marked with crime scene tape, but there was nothing to prevent Nick from using Perry's keys to let himself inside.

Soundlessly, he closed the door behind him. His flashlight played over the empty apartment, spotlighting a half-empty bottle of wine on the coffee table next to an open sketchpad — piercing eyes stared out of the planes and angles of a face that looked suspiciously like his own roughed out in pencil.

He moved to the bedroom. The white beam of the flashlight caught the sexy cartoons of women in exotic dress like a spotlight. The bedclothes were tumbled, the clock on the floor beside the bed. The closet door stood wide, and there was a crooked taped outline where Tiny's body had sprawled as it tumbled from the closet.

Stepping over the taped outline, Nick ran his hands lightly over the back of the closet.

It seemed solid enough. He didn't dare try tapping, despite the temptation to let Center think his buddies in the spirit world were dropping in to say hi. He put his shoulder against it and shoved.

The wall didn't give exactly, but Nick sensed a certain hollowness behind the panel.

Kneeling, he felt along the bottom, and there seemed to be a sharp ridge at the joining of wall and floor. He turned the flashlight on the seam of the wall, following the line and then feeling behind the back shelf at the top of the closet. And there it was. A small spring latch. He pressed it, and the door swung in a few inches, revealing a black mouth of the entrance to what was most definitely a passageway between the rooms.

Nick ran the flashlight over open beams and rough-hewn floors disappearing into darkness.

He felt around, found one of Watson's shoes and stepped into the passageway, stooping long enough to wedge it to keep the doorway from closing all the way shut.

He turned the flashlight ahead, and the back passage seemed to stretch endlessly.

The doorway swung shut with a little click. Nick glanced back. The shoe kept the door from closing all the way. A square of light fell across the wall, illuminating a grimy lantern. Nick turned down the hall, and the square of light grew smaller and smaller behind him.

§ § § §

It was still not light when Perry woke. O'dark hundred, Nick would have said. The clock said five thirty.

For a few moments he lay there, blinking sleepily, trying to place himself in unfamiliar surroundings. He remembered that he was in Nick's bed — without Nick, unfortunately.

And something had wakened him.

There it was again. Perry sat up. He wasn't dreaming. He wasn't imagining that faint scratching sound. Mice in the woodwork? It was only too likely. The only cat in the house was Jane's, and according to Jane, he'd never shown interest in anything that couldn't be opened with a can opener.

There...not exactly a gnawing sound...but...something was moving behind the wall. Something larger than a mouse. Larger than a cat. Something big...

Perry bolted from the bed and made for the living room.

In the murky light he could make out the blankets and pillow neatly folded on the end of the couch. There was no sign of Nick.

Bewildered and still half asleep, Perry tried to make sense of this. He recalled Nick going off to investigate on his own the night Perry had found the dead man in the bathtub. He began to search for his keys. They were gone.

Perry swore. What the hell was the deal with Nick anyway? Would it kill him to ask for help — or at least discuss his plans? For a practical guy, Reno wasn't showing the best sense taking off without making sure he had some kind of backup.

That was probably because he didn't think Perry was much use as backup, and maybe Perry wasn't a Navy SEAL, but he knew enough to get help if Nick needed it.

And if Nick had been gone the entire night, there was a damn good chance he *did* need help.

He went back in the bedroom and dragged on his jeans, stepped into his sneakers, and exited Nick's apartment, leaving the door unlocked just in case he didn't have luck finding Nick.

When he was dressed, he went across the landing to his own tower room just in case Nick was over there, but the door to his apartment was locked — which was doubly annoying. He couldn't get into his own rooms if he wanted to.

Perry went quietly downstairs to the second level. The smell of baking wafted from David Center's rooms, filling the musty hall with warm blueberry fragrance.

Hearing something from the main hall, he looked over the balcony in time to see Miss Dembecki letting herself out the front door, furtive and noiseless. He considered going after her, but the need to find Nick and make sure he was okay was stronger.

He continued quietly down the hallway and studied the imposing crisscross of yellow crime scene tape across Watson's door. Somehow he just knew Nick would not find that forbidding web as intimidating he did.

He tried the handle.

The door swung open.

Perry parted the bands of yellow tape and stepped inside. It was hard to see in the gloom — the blinds drawn against the early morning — and it smelled of the unfamiliar chemicals the crime-scene technicians had used.

"Nick?" he called softly.

There was no answer. He supposed he had not really expected one. Glancing around, he froze at the sight of his open sketchbook — and the rough draft of Nick's face. The deputies must have been looking through his stuff. Hopefully, Nick hadn't seen *that*. He'd be more uncomfortable than he already was.

Perry made his way to the bedroom and snapped on the light, confident that with the blinds drawn no one would be able to tell he was inside the apartment. The closet door stood open.

Something was not right…

At first Perry thought the clothes pole had broken, but then he saw that this was an illusion of the crooked way the shadows fell from the compartment interior. The back wall seemed to be out of alignment.

Cautiously, one eye on the taped outline of where Tiny had died, he stepped inside the closet. Yes, the back wall of the closet was in fact a door. A pretty solid door at that. He felt the edge — four inches thick and solid wood. Something was propping it open. His gaze fell on the shoe wedged between wall and door and his heart stopped.

Cheap brown leather with a hole in the sole. It was the shoe worn by the dead body in Perry's bathtub.

His heart began to thud in tattoo of delighted thrill and alarm.

Just as he had thought — well, suggested — there *was* a secret passage in the house.

Perry pushed against the back panel, taking care not to dislodge the shoe propping it open. Facing what appeared to be a wall of darkness, he paused. He needed a flashlight.

He'd seen one somewhere in Watson's apartment…

Perry ducked back out of the clothes that still smelled of Watson's tobacco and aftershave and searched around until, on the far side of the bed, he finally located a heavy flashlight that looked like it meant business.

Steeling himself, he returned to the closet and pushed the opening wide, stooping long enough to wedge the shoe back into place. He switched on the flashlight.

Long cobwebs floated gently from open beams. Dust coated everything in gray velvet. In fact, he could see a swarm of dusty footprints leading off into the pitch black.

Great. Cold, damp, and dust. The asthma triumvirate. He pulled out his hanky and covered his mouth. He patted the inhaler in his pocket reassuringly. He was okay. He could do this.

Turning the flashlight down the long corridor, Perry began to follow the footsteps in the carpet of dust.

An occasional floorboard squeaked beneath his quiet steps. He was unhappily aware that he and Nick might not be the only people moving through the bowels of the mansion. For sure he now knew how the body of the dead man in his bathtub had been transported away. Someone was using this network of tunnels and walkways as their own private transportation system.

What if Nick had run into that someone? Surely the fact that he had been gone all night was bad news.

As Perry walked he tried to pick out landmarks in case it was difficult to find his way back; it quickly became apparent the narrow tunnels wound through the house like a rabbit warren. How old were they? It seemed that some parts of the passageway were more finished than others indicating that some of the earliest sections might have been part of the original structure while later additions might have happened during the many extensions to the farmhouse — or even at the time of the major renovations of Henry Alston. Certainly these tunnels would have been useful for Alston's parties.

Generations of tunnels…who on the Alston Estate knew about them? Would Mrs. Mac? She had been managing the boarding house for years now. Mr. Teagle was related to the current owners of the house. But did the current owners of the house know about these passageways? Surely when the last renovations had been done — when the reapportioning of rooms for apartments had occurred, the builders would have noticed and mentioned these interior walkways and tunnels.

But if Mr. Teagle and Mrs. Mac knew about these passageways, they had certainly played dumb about them.

Abruptly Perry came to a dead end.

He turned the flashlight on the rough paneling. There it was. A small latch at the top of the door. He pressed it. The door swung backward nearly hitting him. He had a glimpse of a row of silk shirts and tweed jackets in military formation. David Center's closet.

He had somehow managed to travel in a circle. Maybe this explained what Nick had been doing all night.

Perry pressed the latch, closing the door quickly again and started back the other way.

This time he paid closer attention to the direction he was moving, taking note as he passed the band of light that came from Watson's bedroom, crossing through it and continuing to walk for maybe five minutes until he came to a wooden staircase. The passage had narrowed noticeably so that there was just room enough for the stairs leading sharply down into nothingness.

He went down them carefully, counting — fifty steps and then there was a bend and another narrow tunnel — a flat stretch with a stone floor which he traveled quickly — and then more steps leading to another open-beamed walkway like the one on the second floor.

It was much colder down here. He had the impression that he might be outside — underground, perhaps. If he was still inside the house, he had no idea where he was, although he figured he could still find his way back to the house —

From a few yards ahead came the scrape of footsteps. He realized someone was coming toward him. His heart lifted, thinking it was Nick, but then some instinct held him still. He turned out his flashlight and listened.

Would Nick be walking so quickly and confidently?

The footsteps stopped, and Perry heard something…knocking. No…tapping. The person ahead of him was testing the panels, seeking something. Another doorway? A hiding place?

Whatever it was, it gave Perry an opportunity to retreat. Whoever was using these tunnels had probably killed two people already to protect his secret.

As silently as he could, he felt his way, mentally retracing his steps. At this juncture he had made a right…so left now…

He crept along until the sound of tapping died away behind him. Coming to the stairs, he inched quietly up, one hand out to guide himself, one hand gripping the flashlight to use as a possible weapon if he had to.

Unexpectedly reaching the top of the steps, his groping hand touched cloth and then skin. Bright light blazed into his eyes, blinding him momentarily. He put an instinctive hand up, only to be grabbed and thrown back down the stairs.

But the staircase was so narrow that his sprawl of legs and arms worked to stop his headlong crash. Hearing the heavy thud of footsteps following his descent, Perry scrabbled over and half crawled, half fell the rest of the way down the stairs. Reaching the bottom, he jumped up and ran headlong down the passageway only to slam into another compact living form.

Perry cried out.

Hands fastened on his shoulders. "Perry! It's me."

Nick's voice sliced through the panic, and Perry stopped struggling. It *was* Nick. Like the answer to a prayer. It was warmth and strength and safety and everything he'd ever wanted in human form.

Perry's arms locked around the older man. "*Nick.*"

"What's the matter with you?"

Something was the matter, that was for damn sure. Perry babbled a long string of muffled words into Nick's shoulder.

"What? What the hell are you doing down here?" After a hesitation, Nick folded his arms around Perry. "Shh." His lips brushed Perry's ear. It was a small, delicately shaped ear. Reminding Nick of...what? Shells? Scroll work? And it was cold. The kid was shaking like a leaf — and why the hell was he once again not wearing a jacket?

"He tried to kill me," Perry said into his neck.

Nick stilled. "Who?"

"I didn't see. I couldn't tell. He shone his flashlight in my face and then shoved me down the stairs."

Nick was processing fast, preparing for assault even as he said, "Jesus. Are you hurt?" He ran quick hands over Perry's trembling body.

Perry shook his head. "I dropped my flashlight. And my handkerchief."

"Your —" Nick let that go. Perry was walking and conscious, so he was probably okay. Just shaken up. Nick was shaken too — and furious. The thought of that murdering bastard coming after Perry made him want to kill.

He said crisply, "If you're not injured, then pull yourself together." But briefly he gave into temptation and rested his cheek against the soft, spiky hair, before letting Perry go, moving away, drawing his gun. "Stay behind me."

"He could be waiting for us," Perry objected.

"Good," Nick said grimly. "Because I'm sure as hell coming after him." He'd had it with this slippery rat bastard sneaking away through the woodwork every time they got close to him.

He headed for the stairway, moving quietly, keeping well to the side. His night vision was very good, but it was like a cavern down here and all his senses were working to guide him safely.

Once there would have been lanterns hanging from the posts — there were still a few of them, but they had not been touched in years.

His focus was on his quarry, but he was conscious of Perry tagging close on his heels. The kid's breathing had that rushed, strained sound, and Nick knew even before they reached the staircase and found it empty that he needed to abandon mission and get Perry back to warmth and safety.

"Stay here." He took Perry by the arm, moving him safely to the side before turning on his flashlight. He shone the beam around.

Perry's flashlight lay at the bottom of the staircase. The shaft of Nick's flashlight played over the steps. Perry's white hanky lay at the top. There was no sign of anyone.

Whoever their enemy was, he had to be concerned with discovery in a way that they did not. He'd probably already blustered back to his rooms and was setting about making sure everyone in the house knew he was not running around secret passages shoving people down stairwells.

Or he could be lying in wait for them a few yards ahead.

If Nick had been on his own there was no question of what he'd do, but he couldn't risk Perry's safety.

He retrieved Perry's flashlight. "Come on," he whispered and directed the younger man back the way they'd come.

"What is it?" Perry asked, and Nick was obscurely pleased that the kid sounded calm. Tense, but calm. A lot of that was trust in himself, but a lot of it was Perry. He wasn't cut out for this, but he wasn't falling apart, either.

Nick told him, "I think there's a way out down here. I was trying to find the catch when I heard you."

They started back the other way until they came to the spot where Nick had been working before. He shone his flashlight along the wall.

"Feel that draught?" he muttered. "There's a breeze coming through here."

Perry murmured assent.

Nick felt along the top of the panel, but there was no latch.

"There it is," Perry said suddenly, pointing.

Sure enough there was a much more primitive-looking latch close to the bottom of the panel.

"You notice these things have all been cleaned and oiled," he said over his shoulder.

"Yeah," Perry said. "Someone is using these tunnels on a regular basis."

Nick wiggled the latch, pressed, and the door swung out.

They were looking onto a pond inside what appeared to be a tumbling-down barn. There were broken slats in the roof above them. Cold gray daylight left pale rectangles on the still black water. Several large boulders jutted out of the water. Frost powdered the earth ringing the still water.

"We're in the old ice house," Perry said. And then his breath caught raggedly.

Nick shot him a glance, then followed the direction of his stricken gaze. It took an instant for his eyes to make out that long, pale form glimmering in the water.

A man lay facedown in the shallow. His hair was soaked and muddy, he wore a filthy sports coat of yellow and brown plaid checks. Without shoes, his wet feet bobbed gently in their garish yellow socks.

CHAPTER ELEVEN

Perry said very calmly, "Maybe now someone will believe me."

"This ought to do it," Nick agreed. He fastened a hand on Perry's shoulder, guiding him to one of the boulders at the edge of the water. "You stay put; I'm going to call the cops."

Perry, who had started to sit, jumped back up. "I'm not staying here!"

Nick summoned patience. "Someone's got to stay. You want to take the chance of running into your friend from the tunnel?"

Perry wrapped his arms around himself, his expression defiant. "He could show up while you're calling the sheriff."

Nick handed his weapon to Perry. "Here's the safety. You point it and squeeze till the guy stops moving. Aim for the center of him."

Perry took the pistol without looking at it. "Why does anyone have to stay?"

"Because this body disappeared once."

"Let him disappear. I don't care anymore!" Perry's voice wavered. Nick kept his own level.

"Foster, knock it off. Someone's got to stay. I don't have time to argue with you."

That chill tone was like a slap. Perry stared at Nick, then nodded once, tightly.

Nick turned, striding toward the wide wooden door of the icehouse entrance, and pushed on it. It gave a few inches, but then bounced back. Nick swore.

"It'll be locked," Perry informed him tersely. He sat down on the boulder and stared bleakly at the body in the water.

Nick nodded, coming back. He studied Perry and said, "I won't be long."

Perry gave him a long, unfriendly look.

Nick turned and went through the open panel of the secret passage.

It was very quiet after the whisper of his footsteps faded away.

Perry hugged himself against the bitter cold. His breath hung in the dim light. He should have worn a jacket, of course, or at least a sweatshirt, but he hadn't planned on anything like this.

Minutes went by. He tried to look anywhere but at the corpse in the water, but his eyes kept being drawn back to it. He had never seen a dead body before he moved to the Alston Estate. Now he'd seen two in one week.

And less than an hour ago someone had tried to kill him.

Of course, a fall down the stairs wouldn't necessarily kill him, but the intent to do grievous bodily harm had been there — he had felt it.

Now his chest was too tight, and he could feel a cough welling up. He took out his inhaler and puffed, taking a couple of shaky breaths. He was okay, really, just angry with Nick for leaving him here; he was pretty sure the man who had attacked him in the passageway was long gone.

He tried to think if there had been anything to clue him into his attacker. Closing his eyes, he tried to remember those terrifying moments. The light in his eyes had blinded him, but when the man had grabbed him...Perry had an impression of someone taller, certainly broader than he. There had been softness there, though. When he had snatched at the other, trying to prevent himself from falling, he had clutched softness, flab — very different than if he'd grabbed Nick who was all lean, hard muscle. Center was tall and thin — and this person had definitely not been thin.

There had been something else. The smell of tobacco? He wasn't sure. It had been such a transient impression.

How far were they from the main house? Far enough that no one would hear him yelling for help.

The cold and darkness of the icehouse began to press in on him; the soft gurgle of the spring sounded like a dying breath. He began to feel lightheaded, and he pictured himself fainting, falling off his rocky perch, and drowning in the pond. When Nick got back with the sheriff, they could find two corpses — and serve them all right.

In fact, it probably was not more than ten minutes before the chain jangled at the wooden door to the icehouse.

Perry stood, putting aside his inhaler and picking up the pistol, bracing for...he had no idea what.

The door swung back, and Nick stood there in the pallid early morning sunlight.

"Okay?" he called.

"Where is the sheriff?" Perry asked, lowering the pistol. His teeth were starting to chatter.

Nick came around the spring.

"I figured you'd prefer I didn't wait for the sheriff." He shrugged out of his jacket and handed it over to Perry, who took it gratefully, handing over the pistol. "Why the hell didn't you put some kind of sweater on? Kid, are you nuts?"

"I wasn't expecting..." He fumbled his way into the jacket with cold-numbed hands.

Nick shoved the MK23 into the back of his waistband. "Here, zip it up." He reached for Perry, brushing his fingers aside and doing up the zipper. "You have to conserve body heat."

Perry nodded. His chest felt tight and itchy. The longer he spent in this damp cold, the harder it was to breathe, but he was not about to admit that to Nick.

But maybe Nick knew, because he was gazing very seriously into Perry's eyes. His hands were a warm weight on Perry's shoulders, and just for a second they tightened, and Perry thought Nick might kiss him.

Instead, Nick let him go, turning away.

Perry said shortly, "And I'm not a kid, by the way."

"What?"

"You said, 'Kid, are you nuts?' But I'm not a kid. And how nuts was it to go off without telling me — telling anyone — what you were doing last night?"

"How did you find me?" Nick asked, without answering Perry's question.

Perry told him, and Nick said, "Not bad."

"Gee, thanks. But since I found you by accident, I don't think it counts. And by the way, Philip Marlowe," Perry continued shortly, "the shoe you used to prop the doorway open was the one from my room. The one *he* was wearing." He nodded to the corpse floating in the water.

"Are you shitting me?" Nick's chagrin was some consolation.

"Yeah, don't feel too bad," Perry said kindly. "After all, you only saw it the one time."

Of course, Perry had only seen it the one time, too. Nick opened his mouth, caught Perry's gaze, and snorted. "Smart ass."

And Perry felt a little better.

It took the sheriff's department half an hour to show up. They turned out with enough personnel to take in Bonnie and Clyde, uniforms flooding into the ramshackle building, shouting directions to each other and then countermanding the directions with more directions.

Perry and Nick were escorted outside and questioned — if you could call it questioning. Sheriff Butler was on the defensive, having dismissed the original finding of the body — and for not having noticed there was a hidden door in the closet where the other dead man had been found.

"You're sure you don't know the victim?" he asked Perry for the third time.

"I don't know him. I never saw him before he showed up in my bathtub."

"Why pick *your* bathtub do you think?"

Perry replied patiently, "Because I was supposed to be out of town."

Butler had obviously forgot this little fact, and the fact that it irritated him showed in the clipped way he ordered Nick to present the opening to the secret passage.

Nick led Butler back through the icehouse, and the sheriff and his deputies swarmed inside the tunnel to investigate.

"Let's go," Nick said to Perry stepping outside again.

The sun was making a determined effort to throw a little feeble warmth over the muddy yard. A thrush — late in leaving for the winter — was singing sweetly from the middle of a thicket.

Perry and Nick walked back to the house. Perry said — not with any great conviction — "That should be the end of it, don't you think?"

Nick shook off his preoccupation. "How do you figure that?"

"Well, whoever this lunatic is, he'll have to give up now."

"I don't think he's going to give up. He's killed two people so far."

"But now that everyone knows about the tunnels — now that the sheriff knows —"

Nick said grimly, "I hate to burst your bubble, but the cops are liable to start suspecting you."

"*Me?*"

"People who discover bodies are always suspects."

"Why would they be?"

"Because pretending to find somebody's body after you've just killed them is one of the oldest tricks in the book."

Perry said nothing, frowning as he thought it over.

"Look at from the view of the sheriff's department," Nick said. "There are a lot of suspicious coincidences here. The dead guy was originally in your apartment —"

"But no one believed me."

"Then you find Tiny. He practically dies in your arms."

"But he'd been shot hours earlier. Maybe even the day before."

"No one saw him after he let you into Watson's apartment."

"But you were with me."

Nick shrugged.

"Why would I kill Tiny? Why would I kill anyone? I don't have a motive. Or a gun."

"Motive is a secondary consideration. The cops look for means and opportunity first."

"That doesn't make any sense. Motive is the most important thing. I don't have any *reason* to want someone dead."

Nick said calmly, "Motive is too subjective. What one person considers a good reason to kill might not make sense to someone else. There are people who kill because they don't want to lose custody of their children or split their assets or go to jail for embezzling or because they get caught burgling a house or because they want someone else's wife — or car."

Perry bit his lip. "You think I'm really a suspect?"

Nick glanced at him. Perry's profile was uncharacteristically hard. "Only if they're complete idiots — but I haven't seen any proof that they're not."

Perry nodded wearily, and Nick thought, *Oh, what the hell.* He put his arm around Perry's shoulders and gave him a hard, brief hug.

The smile Perry gave him almost took his breath away. But when Perry spoke, it was mundane enough. "What do you think those jewels would be worth now?"

Nick shook his head. "If it was a fortune in jewels then, I guess it would be a king's ransom now. That stuff appreciates considerably. Assuming, wherever this loot has been stashed, it's still intact."

Perry knew Nick was thinking that the jewels might be at the bottom of the spring in the icehouse — or scattered through the garden and woods. Anything was possible.

§ § § §

They returned to Nick's apartment, and Nick went immediately to the kitchen to start breakfast.

"Is it okay if I take a shower?" Perry asked. His chest had that constricted, scratchy feeling again, but he didn't want to use his inhaler too much — he couldn't afford to replace it anytime soon, and he only had about fifty sprays left in it. The way things were going, he could use that easily in the next day or two.

"Help yourself," Nick said.

The steam helped, or maybe it was just the soothing warmth of the water. Guiltily, Perry lingered longer than he should have, using all Nick's hot water, but when he left the bathroom in a cloud of steam, he felt much better — though exhausted.

They had breakfast — pancakes that morning — spread with real butter and drenched in the rich maple syrup for which Vermont was justly famous.

They talked desultorily, and then Nick said, "I'm going to grab some rack time. Why don't you go back to bed for a while?"

Perry opened his mouth to suggest that if Nick wanted to keep an eye on him, they could share the bed — that quick hug earlier and the way he'd caught Nick looking at him lately made him hopeful that Nick might be more receptive than he'd originally thought — but Nick was wearing his tough guy face, his thoughts clearly elsewhere, and Perry wasn't sure he was feeling up to that particular rejection.

It occurred to him that he had managed to go over twenty-four hours without even thinking of Marcel. But if the solution for Marcel was Nick, the cure might be worse than the disease.

Perry slept uneasily — he was never one for taking naps or sleeping during the day — and he woke from a dream that he was back in the passage facing down that blazing light. Only this time the light was followed by a gunshot.

He sat up.

Rising from the bed, he went into the living room. Nick was wrapped in a blanket. His face was smooth and enigmatic in sleep. His arms were folded across his chest — as self-contained as one of those ancient Egyptian kings settling down for a long winter's nap. Perry studied him curiously.

Nick's eyes snapped open, and he reached for the pistol beneath his pillow before he realized it was Perry standing over him.

"What are you doing?" He lowered the pistol.

Feeling like a fool, Perry got out, "I was just checking to see if you were awake."

"Next time try, 'Hey, Nick, are you awake?' You're less likely to get your head blown off." But despite the growl, Nick didn't really seem annoyed. He yawned hugely and sat up.

Perry was still standing there uncertainly. "Couldn't you sleep?" Nick asked.

"I don't sleep in the day unless I'm sick."

"Okay. Well…" Nick yawned again and shook himself. "Why don't we go outside before the rain starts again and try some target practice."

"What?"

Nick's deep blue eyes met the younger man's. "I want you to be able to defend yourself if you have to."

Perry was instantly on defense; Nick was beginning to recognize the signs. "From what? Miss Dembecki? I don't think I'm going to get in an extended firefight in this house."

Nick uncoiled in one of those swift moves. "Look, two people have been killed. What do you plan on doing if this asshole comes after you again? He could just as easily have —"

He broke off as someone knocked on the door. "Hang on," he said, and moved to answer it. Mr. Teagle stood in the doorway, looking uncomfortable.

"I was looking for —" Seeing Perry, he broke off. "There you are, son. I was worried about you. No one seemed to know where you were."

"He's staying with me for now," Nick said.

Mr. Teagle looked even more uncomfortable — and unhappy. Instead of answering Nick, he said to Perry, "Could I have a word in private, son?"

Perry, feeling harassed on all sides, managed not to sigh — which was more than Nick managed as he stepped aside to let Perry pass into the hall with Mr. Teagle. He closed the door politely and pointedly on them.

Perry controlled his impatience. "What's wrong, Mr. Teagle?" he asked politely, shoving his hands into pockets.

Mr. Teagle cleared his throat — a less-than-charming sound. "I'm just not comfortable with this arrangement of yours, Perry," he said earnestly, turning the thick horn-rims on Perry. "What do you know about this young fella, Reno? There's some mighty peculiar things been happening in this house lately."

Of all the things Perry had expected…

"Nick isn't responsible for any of the weird things happening," he assured Mr. Teagle wearily. "This all started long before Nick arrived here."

"How do you work that out? Since that young fella arrived we've had *two* murders. Now it doesn't take a genius to see that there's more to all this than meets the eye."

Perry puzzled over that comment for a moment. Wasn't it a given that there was more than met the eye to any violent death?

He said, "I think whatever is going on in this house has been going on long before Nick showed up."

Mr. Teagle licked his lips. "You're too trusting, Perry," he said quite sternly. "I feel responsible with your parents so far away. I want you to come and stay with me until we get this all ironed out. I've got a bad feeling about that young fella."

Perry felt an irrational rush of anger. Irrational because Nick would just laugh this bullshit off; he didn't need Perry running to his defense. In fact, for all Perry knew, Nick might be only too happy to foist him off on Mr. Teagle.

He said stiffly, "Thanks, Mr. Teagle, but I feel perfectly safe staying with Nick. We've already worked everything out." Which meant pretty much nothing, but Mr. Teagle's face got red.

"I don't think you understand about men like that," he said with uncomfortable urgency. "They prey on youngsters like yourself. They take...advantage. They don't...cherish innocence."

Perry started to point out that at twenty-three he was hardly a youngster, but as he stared at Mr. Teagle's anxious face, the light began to dawn.

"Uh, thanks for your concern," he said awkwardly, "but it's not necessary." He was tempted to shock the old man and say he wasn't all that innocent, but unfortunately that wouldn't have been true. And Mr. Teagle meant well. Maybe he wasn't even completely aware of his own motives.

Compelled by instinct he hadn't had time to explore, he said, "Mr. Teagle, you knew all about the hidden passages in the house, didn't you? You've known for years."

Mr. Teagle turned the color of his freckles and then went white.

What on earth...? And then Perry knew. All those times he'd had that uncomfortable feeling of being watched, of being not alone —

His mouth dropped open, and he stared at Mr. Teagle. There was no concealing his honest shock and dismay, and the old man said quickly, querulously, "It's nothing like that, nothing like what you think! I have a responsibility to keep an eye on what happens in this house. That's all."

"You were w-watching me!" Perry stammered.

Mr. Teagle blustered out something else about Perry's imagination and having a duty to make sure people were behaving themselves, but Perry missed it because by then he had retreated into Nick's apartment and slammed the door.

Nick was in the kitchen sipping his coffee when he heard the door slam. A moment later, Perry walked in. One glance at his face told Nick that he still had his bunkmate. He didn't analyze his pleasure in this because he noticed that Perry was quite white.

"What's the matter? What did he say to you?" Nick was on his feet, ready to do battle — another feeling he didn't dare explore too carefully.

"He's been watching me," Perry said, and he sounded genuinely shaken. "He knew all about those hidden walkways, and he's been using them to keep track of everyone. He's some kind of a Peeping Tom."

"He admitted that to you? Did he say he killed —"

If Teagle was their killer — Nick considered that objectively. The old man had knowledge of the tunnels. He wasn't in good health and couldn't lug a man the size of Tiny or the unknown corpse in the icehouse far, but he wouldn't necessarily have to since he'd know how to play Chutes and Ladders through the mansion. He was also related to the family that now owned the Alston Estate, which meant there was a very good chance he knew all about the Alston sapphires and Shane Moran.

And to top it off, he was a creep.

But Perry was shaking his head. "No. Nothing like that. He just admitted he knew about the passageways. He gave me some bullshit story about having a duty to keep an eye on everyone…but… *Nick!*"

The youthful protest in that got Nick like no righteous indignation would have.

"Don't worry, I'll have a word with him," he said grimly, on his way to the doorway. "That shit stops here and now. And when I get done with him he can explain to the cops what he was doing prowling around —"

But Perry grabbed his arm, and somehow Nick couldn't pull away from him. Instead, he returned Perry's hug, putting his arms stiffly around him.

"I knew it," Perry said. "I knew there was something weird. I could feel it sometimes when I was getting undressed or" — he moaned — "when I was jacking off."

The picture *that* conjured raised an entirely inappropriate response from Nick's body. A response that was pretty damn difficult to hide what with Perry clutching him and inarticulately mumbling his embarrassment into Nick's neck.

If Teagle wasn't a murderer, then in the greater scheme of things it wasn't really that traumatic — some lonely old perv copping a peek through the bathroom wall — but Perry was about as sheltered as they came these days, and clearly he felt violated on all kinds of levels.

So Nick tried to ease his erection out of Perry's groin while not actually breaking free, because Perry apparently required a hug, and it was unexpectedly important to Nick that Perry get what he needed when he needed it.

"Yeah, I know. But it's done and you're okay," Nick told him. He meant to say it bracingly, but it came out soft and coaxing. It was a tone he couldn't remember ever having used before on anyone — certainly not with Marie, certainly not in the rough and mostly silent encounters with his occasional casual lovers.

Perry raised an indignant face. "And he had the balls to tell me I should stay with him, because we didn't know anything about *you*!"

Nick laughed and gave in to the urge to brush Perry's fair hair out of his eyes — his fingertips sensitive to the silky texture of eyebrows and hair, warm skin, eyelashes.

Perry's lashes fluttered down, concealing his eyes.

"Hey," Nick said huskily.

Perry gave him an uncertain look.

It was a mistake, of course. A huge mistake. But suddenly, urgently Nick wanted to taste Perry's mouth, so he bent his head. Perry's eyes widened, then their faces bumped, and his mouth found Perry's.

It was a gentle kiss, because Nick was thinking what a stupid thing this was to do, and that Perry, being inexperienced, would probably expect songbirds and firecrackers.

Perry tasted like hot chocolate and something warm and young and male. It was unexpectedly erotic. He responded sweetly, opening right up, and Nick's heart turned over in his chest.

His hands slid down Perry's back, feeling delicate bones and tension, warm nakedness beneath too many clothes. And, without thinking anymore, his hands went to Perry's waistband. He was amused and titillated to feel Perry's hands mimicking the motions of his own. The kid's knuckles felt feverish against Nick's belly as he fumbled with Nick's belt. His expression was dead serious, which touched Nick in some unused corner of his heart.

"Let's take this below deck," he said, and he scooped Perry up over his shoulder. Perry burst out laughing, head dangling down at Nick's waistband. He tried to raise up, and Nick smacked his ass.

Nick carried him into the bedroom and flung him down on his back on the bed. Perry was still laughing, a kid's untroubled laugh. There was trust in the fawn eyes that pierced Nick right through some vulnerable piece of his anatomy there really wasn't a name for.

Perry was nearly his own height; small framed but not badly built for being so slight. His cock sprang up like a cadet eager for training.

"At ease, son. You don't have to salute," Nick told him, and Perry gave that endearing giggle. Nick pounced on the bed and crouched over him. Perry reached up and ran his hand through Nick's crisp, short cut.

"Like porcupine quills," he said. "Only soft." He smiled. "You have the bluest eyes I ever saw."

"The better to see you with."

Perry's lips quivered. "My, Grandma, what white teeth you have."

"The better to eat you with," Nick said and proceeded to demonstrate.

Perry was...delectable. Sweet and shivering beneath Nick's onslaught, moaning softly as Nick nibbled and nipped, keeping him writhing in desperate pleasure. But Nick miscalculated Perry's excitement — and experience — and the sudden eruption of slippery hot silk between their bodies took them both by surprise.

Nick drew back to study the mistimed fusillade.

"Goddamn it!" Perry said, sounding so chagrined that Nick laughed.

"It's all right. Plenty more where that came from." And at Perry's age, it was true. As Nick's tongue traced the damp pulse of Perry's femoral artery, Perry was gasping, his body already beginning to respond in slow, sensual movements.

Nick took his time — anything worth doing was doing right — and he wanted Perry's first real experience to be the very best it could be, so he applied the tactics he'd learned with Marie. Little tricks with tongue and lips he'd never have dreamed of using on another guy — not in the kind of impersonal sexual encounters he typically favored — but they made Perry wild.

Something to make note of for another place and time, but oddly enough, Nick didn't want to consider another place and time. Right now, showing and sharing with Perry seemed the only thing that really mattered.

Perry's thin, artist's hands clutched Nick's shoulders, and he was getting hard again, moving against Nick in urgent little thrusts — surprisingly, enjoyably uninhibited.

Nick took the head of the kid's cock into his mouth, tasting that salt and sweet, and Perry arched up, making inarticulate sounds Nick unexpectedly found exciting. He drew the long, thin shaft in, sucking Perry hard and then easy, taking him in deeply, maneuvering his way down to the kid's silky groin, which smelled pleasantly of boy sweat and semen.

Perry raised his head and watched himself disappearing in and out of Nick's wet, hard mouth, and he made a long, keening sound, dropped his head back in the pillow, and began to ejaculate in creamy spurts.

Nick had known by the way Perry's belly clenched, the way his thighs squeezed, what was happening — he probably knew before Perry did. There was time to move out of the line of fire, but he found that he didn't want to. He wanted to do this for Perry — and he wanted to do it for himself — and he swallowed the warm, wet burst of orgasm.

By then Nick's need had reached boiling point, and he lowered himself on top of Perry's shuddering frame and ground against him, his swollen, throbbing dick finding relief in the friction of velvety skin and the hard, close press of bodies. He'd timed it just about right, and it didn't take any time at all before his own release was shooting between them, slick and hot.

"Oh *God*, Nick," Perry said. It was practically the only thing he'd said the entire time, and it was disarmingly heartfelt.

Nick collapsed on him, and Perry fastened a tight arm around his back and kissed him on his ear and his temple and his hair. *Puppy kisses*, Nick thought. *Puppy love...*

§ § § § §

Perry surfaced. He was warm and sticky and utterly, deliciously relaxed. From the other room he could hear Nick talking quietly. The phone? California calling again? He frowned a little, thinking about what would happen when Nick left.

That would be hard. He'd have to tough it out somehow. Nick would never have patience with him getting all weepy and clinging, and he wanted to spend every possible minute with Nick before he left.

He'd need those memories to hold to all the long, lonely nights that would follow Nick's departure.

Hearing the murmur of a second voice, he realized Nick wasn't on the phone. He sat up, pulled on his jeans. Found his shirt. His hair was sticking up on end. He combed his fingers through it, walking down the short hallway.

"She could be a danger — not just to herself but to the rest of us. I mean, if she's going around hitting people over the head —" Jane broke off what she was saying to greet Perry. "Well, there you are. How are you feeling after your morning's adventure?"

For a minute he thought she was referring to what he and Nick had done. Then sanity reasserted itself. "Good." Perry couldn't look at Nick. He was afraid his face would give him away.

"You look better than I expected. There's a little color in your cheeks."

He couldn't help it; he raised his gaze. Nick's eyes held his for a second, and Perry knew that now there was even more color in his face. Nick's face was blank. He was probably great at poker. Perry was great at Old Maid.

"There's cocoa in the kitchen," Nick said laconically.

"Oh. Thanks."

He stepped into the kitchen, poured cocoa while listening to Jane. She called out, "Miss Dembecki has just confessed to hitting Mr. Stein over the head with a poker."

Perry stepped back out of the kitchen. "You're…kidding."

Jane shook her head. "Nope. I was helping her with her laundry, and she just casually mentioned it, just as breezy as could be. She said she thought he was a burglar."

"But…" He looked to Nick who shrugged. "Why…what was she doing in my apartment?"

Jane shook her head. "I have no idea. I'm not sure she does. She's getting very…peculiar is all I can say. And if she's starting to whack people over the heads with pokers…"

Perry said to Nick, "But how did we miss her going downstairs?"

"I guess if she hit him and ran — we didn't look over the balcony, we just went across to your place and then went inside."

"But the deputy would have seen her."

Nick's lip curled. "I knew that deputy was full of shit about how long he was away from his post."

Jane said, "And that's not all, by the way. The cops claim they've identified your body."

Perry turned away from Nick. "Really? Who is he?"

"An investigator out of Jersey," Nick said. "Raymond Swiss."

"A private eye? For real? Why was he in my bathtub? Do they know who he was working for?"

Jane responded. "If the cops know, they're not telling us lowly civilians. Apparently his secretary filed a missing persons report on him Monday when he didn't return to the office."

"He was a long way from home." Perry digested this. "So...he was killed in this house?"

"It could have been an accident." Jane hugged herself against a sudden chill. "But that's the thing. They're saying he died from a blow to the head."

"You're not thinking Miss Dembecki?" Perry protested.

"She's not denying she clobbered Mr. Stein. The thing is the cops have taken Mr. Teagle in for questioning." Jane was eyeing Nick speculatively. "And that was after your friend here had a word with them."

Perry swallowed. He didn't like to think of poor Mr. Teagle in jail even if he was an old weirdo. He couldn't believe that he was a murderer, although he clearly had a few issues. But he couldn't believe Miss Dembecki had killed someone, either.

He said, "If it was an accident, why didn't someone say?"

Jane shrugged. "Maybe they didn't know what they were doing. Maybe they still don't." She added slowly, "Maybe they were afraid. Maybe...they couldn't come forward."

Perry stared at her trying to follow this reasoning.

"Nobody killed Tiny by accident," he said. "Tiny was shot."

Nick said, "From the way you described the body, I'm guessing Swiss had been dead for a while by the time he was stashed in your apartment. He was probably killed somewhere else in the house. Maybe the basement. No one but Tiny ever went down there, and it would be pretty easy to clean up."

"Or maybe he was killed in one of the secret tunnels," Jane said. "They run all through the house and through the grounds and — get this, it's pretty awful — there are all kind of eyeholes and listening stations throughout the house."

As though on cue, there was a scratching sound behind the fireplace wall.

"They're in the woodwork," Jane muttered. "Cops, I mean. They've been prowling through the passages all morning."

Perry gulped, thinking about all those peepholes. Meeting his eyes, Nick grimaced. The same thought had apparently crossed his mind.

Jane said, "Then whoever killed Tiny must have killed him to cover up the original crime — whether it was an accident or not." She looked pale. "You'd have to be pretty ruthless to kill someone as harmless as Tiny."

"Yeah," Nick said. "I think we're dealing with someone pretty ruthless. It would be a good idea not to forget it."

CHAPTER TWELVE

When Jane finally talked out her nervousness and departed, Nick said, "Okay, we've still got enough daylight to get in some target practice. Grab your jacket."

Perry stiffened. He said shortly, "Look, I already know how to use a gun."

"Great," Nick said easily. "Then this won't take long."

"Not long at all, because I'm not going shooting."

Nick raised his brows at this open defiance. Perry was obviously scared to death of firearms — which was pretty much what he had expected.

He said patiently, "I need to know that you can take care of yourself, and I don't think hand-to-hand combat is going to be your thing."

"Neither is shooting people."

Nick choked back his immediate retort. He said mildly, "I'm not asking you to become a sniper, but if you get cornered by your pal from the passageway again, you might find this useful." He offered his backup weapon, a Sig P-228. Small, light, accurate, and easy to conceal, all of which made it a perfect choice for Perry.

Except Perry was not cooperating. He stared at the Sig, not moving. His eyes raised to Nick's. The Bambi look.

Nick hardened his heart. "I want you to carry it till this thing gets straightened out."

Perry lifted one shoulder. "Fine." He still hadn't touched the gun.

"But first I want to be sure you know how to use it."

"I already said."

"I want to see for myself."

Perry flushed, his eyes narrowing. "You won't take my word for it?"

His righteous affront took Nick by surprise. He said quickly, "Yeah, I take your word for it, but I want to see whether you can hit anything."

Perry put down his cocoa and rose from the table. "Fine. Whatever. Let's just get this over with."

He was still not speaking as they climbed into Nick's pickup. Nick told himself he was unmoved. The kid could sulk all he liked. This was for his own good. Like learning to eat properly or wearing a condom.

But better not to let his thoughts drift in that direction, or they'd be heading straight back into the house for a little more afternoon delight. It was disconcerting. Nick hadn't felt like this…well, it had been a long time. He wasn't sure he'd ever exactly felt like this, because he was uncomfortably aware that he was taking advantage here. Cradle robbing, that's what they called it. That was one of the nicer things they called it.

He drove until they passed a long empty meadow. Nick pulled to the side of the road, and they walked out through the tall grass. Nick lined up a row of tin cans he'd liberated from the recycling bin before they left the house.

He walked back to where Perry waited, hands shoved in his jean pockets, an un-Perry-like scowl on his pointed face.

Nick demonstrated. "Okay. Here's the clip. You —"

Perry took the clip from him and slapped it into the P-228. He turned, stepped into perfect firing stance, and fired off three rounds.

Nick blinked as *blam, blam, blam* the tin cans went flying one after another off the crumbled stone wall.

"Jesus, Foster. You've got a hell of an eye…"

Perry fired off four more rounds. Clean, accurate shots picking off the rest of the tin cans. He ejected the clip and handed the empty Sig Sauer to Nick. He gave him that long, unfriendly look Nick had seen once before when Perry felt he had been seriously let down.

"Where the hell —"

"I learned to shoot when I was ten. My dad thought it was important for a man to be able to handle himself, which according to him meant being able to use a gun. I can blow away tin cans all day, and we both know that it doesn't mean anything against a live target."

He was right. Again. It was beginning to be a habit with him.

Nick finally found his voice. "Fair enough. But at least I know you can hit something if you have to."

Perry shook his head. "I couldn't shoot someone. No way."

Nick strove for patience. Perry was coming at this from a perspective alien to his. "You don't think if your life was in danger…"

"My dad used to make me go hunting with him. He said…" Perry changed his mind about sharing whatever recollection that was. Instead, he said, "I shot a rabbit once. It screamed."

"They do sometimes," Nick admitted.

"I threw up."

"Look, frankly, I don't get a big kick out of hunting, either," Nick said. "There's a difference —"

"I'm going back to the truck." Perry stalked away.

§ § § §

Miss Dembecki greeted them when they returned to the house. She looked, to Perry's uneasy eye, like she hadn't combed her hair for a couple of days — or changed her clothes.

What happened to people like Miss Dembecki once they couldn't take care of themselves? She didn't seem to have any family.

She clutched his sleeve, saying eagerly, "Isn't it dreadful! These secret passages run all through the house." But her eyes were bright with excitement, not alarm.

"You've lived here so long," Perry said. "Didn't you have any idea about the secret passages?"

"Oh no! None of us knew. Not even Mrs. Mac."

Well, that was clearly not true. Mr. Teagle had already plainly, if inadvertently, admitted to knowing about the tunnels.

Tiny might have known — he'd been prowling the estate for decades. Certainly the back passages had served in his mysterious disappearance. He didn't appear to have been killed in the house. It was possible, though not probable, that he could have been dragged into the passage against his will. But surely someone would have seen or heard something?

Then again, Raymond Swiss had disappeared in this house — presumably against his will — and no one had seen or heard anything. Except his murderer.

And that was a point right there. Surely no one was going to be willing to admit to prior knowledge of the secret passages, because it automatically made them a suspect in Tiny's and Swiss's killings. And the fact that Mr. Teagle's concern had been over being caught out peeping surely meant he hadn't been worried about being suspected of murder because he hadn't committed murder?

As though reading his mind, Miss Dembecki said, "The police have discovered where Tiny was shot in the passageway. They think his killer must have thought he was dead and left him, and then Tiny must have dragged himself to the door that leads into Mr. Watson's apartment. And then he was too weak to go any farther."

Nick asked, "Do they have any leads on who might have shot him? Have they narrowed the weapon down?"

"Oh! They've been searching for guns in poor Mr. Teagle's rooms." Miss Dembecki fluttered away and then — as Perry and Nick started up the staircase — fluttered back. "They've arrested him, you know. Mr. Teagle."

§ § § §

They ate at the kitchen table. Framed in the window over the sink, an enormous orange half moon seemed to be dissolving right out of the black night.

Nick had roasted a chicken for dinner, and he served it with mashed potatoes, gravy, and corn. The food was good —

everything Nick cooked was good — but Perry picked at his supper.

Watching him, Nick's brows drew together. "Eat."

They hadn't talked since they'd returned from target practice. Nick assumed Perry was sulking, and he had no intention of giving into that, but...he missed the easy companionship. He was getting used to it, getting used to Perry being around. Perry looked up. "I can't when I'm nervous."

Unimpressed, Nick said, "You're always nervous. You need to replenish your nervous energy."

Perry nodded, picked some more at his food.

Nick sighed. "What's on your mind?"

He thought he had a pretty good idea, so he was taken off stride when Perry said, "That was true about your wife, right? You were really married?"

"Hell yes, I was married."

"But you…"

Nick gazed into the Bambi eyes and said harshly, "Are you asking if you were the first guy I've been with? Don't be dumb."

Perry's eyes darkened. His mouth went soft and hurt before he managed to control his face. Stonily, he said, "I didn't think you learned those moves by osmosis. I just wondered if you considered yourself gay or what."

Nick nearly laughed at the osmosis comment, but he realized that if he laughed at Perry now, it could likely end here. And maybe that would be the wisest thing — the best thing for Perry before this went any further, and the kid did something silly like convince himself he was in love — but Nick found he couldn't do it.

He said calmly, "Yes. I'm gay. I married when I was younger than you are now. I didn't think I had a choice back then."

"And then…?"

It was obvious Perry didn't know what questions to ask, and Nick said a little more gently, "I grew up. I learned that there were other choices and other ways to live."

Perry was watching him steadily. Nick sighed. "Marie — my ex — and I knew we'd made a mistake within a couple of years. She found her way of dealing with it and I found mine. I wasn't always as careful as I should have been, and it resulted in" — Nick took a deep breath. This was still hard to admit even to himself — "me getting kicked out of the navy."

"They fucking dishonorably discharged *you*?" Perry's shocked outrage was unexpectedly sweet. The kid's eyes were bright with anger — too bright — and Nick recognized with a jolt that for the first time in his entire life someone was about to shed tears on his behalf.

"Hey, hey." He reached out and covered Perry's fist where it lay on the scrubbed oak table. "Listen, I was stupid. I knew the risk. I thought it was worth it, and I'm not going to kick now." He gave Perry's thin hand a squeeze and let it go. He was surprised to find himself smiling. "It's okay. I'm okay."

"Yeah." Perry expelled a breath. "Bastards," he said fiercely.

Nick laughed — and about something he never thought he'd laugh about. "Eat your dinner, Foster. I don't like my hard work going to waste."

§ § § §

After dinner, Nick looked over the brochures for his training curriculum — which included everything from courses in computer research to report writing — and Perry went across to his apartment to get another sketchpad. He settled on the floor across from the sofa trying to watch Nick without being too obvious about it.

After a minute or two, though, Nick looked up. There was a glint in his gaze that warned Perry Nick had seen the sketch he had begun from memory at Watson's.

"You're wasting your talent on a mug like mine," Nick informed him.

Perry said, "You've got a great face."

Nick reddened and returned to his reading without comment. Perry sketched for a while — it gave him the excuse to stare at Nick as much as he liked. It was clear that Nick was totally absorbed in his reading, looking forward to California and his new job — his new life.

"I'm going to get some fresh air," Perry said, laying the pad aside.

Nick looked up then. "Take the Sig and stick close to the house."

Perry grimaced. "I can't see that there would be any danger at this point. Everyone and their grandmother knows about the tunnels now."

"We don't know why Raymond Swiss was killed, and we're guessing that Tiny was killed because of his big mouth. We could be totally off the track on all of this. And even if we're not, neither death necessarily has a damn thing to do with Shane Moran's missing loot."

"What else could they all be looking for? Dembecki searching the gazebo and Rudy Stein checking out local history around that period?"

"Dembecki is unraveling faster than a ball of yarn, and Teagle, who did know about the passageways, turns out to have been interested in a different kind of jewels."

Perry made a face. "Don't remind me."

Nick grinned, his face unexpectedly young in the soft lamplight. "Just sayin'."

"Yeah, well *don't.*"

Nick laughed.

"And what about Stein?" Perry asked. "He was doing all that research on this area back in the thirties."

"That doesn't prove anything."

"We could ask him what he was researching," Perry suggested.

He was half kidding, but Nick said thoughtfully, "Yeah, we could at that."

Then, apparently losing interest, Nick returned to his reading.

Perry went downstairs and walked briefly around the front yard, sticking close to the house. The pistol in his jacket pocket was awkward and heavy. He felt ridiculous wearing it. No way could he shoot someone. Nick just didn't get it.

Irritably, he glanced back at the house and saw Nick's figure outlined in the window of the tower — watching him. Perry's irritation melted in foolish warmth.

§ § § §

When Perry returned upstairs, Nick was unfolding the blanket on the couch.

He glanced over his shoulder and said brusquely, "You can take the bed again. I may decide to take another look around later." As Perry opened his mouth to object, he continued, "This is what I'm trained for, okay?"

So that was pretty clear. They were not sharing a bed. This afternoon had been…well, whatever it had been, it clearly wasn't going to be a regular thing.

"Okay," Perry said. "Good night."

"Night," Nick said curtly.

Perry went into Nick's bedroom and changed into his pajamas. He sat down on the edge of the bed and listened to Nick moving around in the other room. Then the lights went off.

He sat there for a few minutes more, and then he went down the hallway.

"Nick?"

Nick's form rose up from the sofa, a dark shadow moving through the other shadows. "What's wrong?" The warm weight of his hands rested on Perry's shoulders. Perry's heart ached, thinking of the skillful and pleasurable things Nick's hands had done to him earlier that day.

Never again?

"I just thought…there's plenty of room in that bed."

Nick was very still, his breath warm against Perry's flushed face.

He said quietly, flatly, "Listen, Perry, I'm leaving in a week or so. I won't be back."

"I know." Perry smiled with an effort — he didn't know if Nick could see his face in the quicksilver moonlight, but he hoped he heard it in his voice. "No strings. It's just sex."

There was a funny pause. Nick said, "It sounds wrong when you say it like that."

Perry didn't — couldn't — say anything.

He could feel Nick's hesitation — but not reluctance, surely? Nick said, "I just want us to be on the same map."

"Absolutely," Perry assured him.

Still Nick didn't move. Then he said slowly. "You're taking this better than I expected."

"I like sleeping with you," Perry said. "I don't want to waste time talking."

§ § § § §

And they did not talk. Nick was laconic by nature and Perry was shy — and adrift in unfamiliar sensation and emotions. They communicated by touch. Not the gentle, enlightening caresses of that afternoon; this was more urgent, more intense, partly perhaps because it had been a near miss. It still might be the last time.

Nick's body covered Perry's, and he could feel Perry's fast and frantic heartbeats against his chest. Fast as the frightened pound of something small and gentle — a rabbit or a fawn. But when he pulled back to study Perry's face, he could see the shine of Perry's eyes and the gleam of his teeth, and he was smiling, not scared, just excited. Nick's mouth covered Perry's, and Perry's lips were warm and soft and welcoming. His breath was light and fast, and it seemed suddenly, strangely precious to Nick.

A surge of unexpected emotion tempered his — considerable — lust.

He gathered Perry to him closely, warmly, feeling velvet soft skin and the silky hair of Perry's chest and groin. Perry wrapped his arms around Nick, holding him back tightly, opening up to Nick's kiss — Nick didn't generally kiss other men, but somehow it was different with Perry. He liked his taste, he liked the softness and eagerness with which he responded to the press of mouths. He stroked him, enjoying the touch of strong bone beneath thin, delicate skin, and Perry murmured approval.

Nick settled between Perry's legs, Perry moving instinctively to accommodate him, and again he sensed no anxiety as they rocked together. Perry was turned on and right there with Nick as their bodies changed pace, temperatures rising. Perry's cock was prodding Nick's belly and Nick's cock...

He told himself to slow down...although Perry was making it difficult for him as his mouth latched onto one of Nick's nipples, turning it pebble hard with a flick of his tongue. Perry's mouth was trailing down the taut line of Nick's throat, the muscular planes of his chest. *Go slow*, Nick warned himself, because Perry was all theory and imagination, and the reality was a bit more painful.

He wrapped an arm around Perry and rolled over so that now Perry was on top. He could feel the younger man's surprise. Nick was a little surprised himself, but he stroked Perry, kneaded his ass cheeks, again taking time, reassuring by touch. With his free hand he reached for the lube, applying it liberally to that tight — very tight — little hole, turning this into something sensuous.

Perry's initial stiffness melted away, and even when Nick unwrapped the latex, there was no discernable anxiety, no second thoughts. They fell back into the rhythm, lulled by the drive of longing, the pulse of desire, Nick was as careful as he knew how to be, pushing slowly but steadily at the wall of resistance.

Perry panted and then whimpered, but he didn't retreat — he pushed down onto Nick's cock — stubborn, insistent, shivering with a mix of wanting and hurting — and then Nick was in. And not moving, not taking was one of the most difficult things he'd ever done. He held himself in check, taking the time to soothe and pamper until it was Perry who initiated, a little awkwardly, but Nick met him, let him set the pace, and soon they were caught up again in that frantic tempo, the push and pull, the drag and draw, that slow, delicious friction rapidly building to something frantic and ferocious until at last they tumbled off the edge into the deep end of ecstasy.

They found themselves at last leaden limbed and catching their breath on the beach of a new uneasy understanding.

§ § § §

Let the journey begin, the faded, peeling billboard read. A young man in dress uniform gazed keen-eyed into a future that had surely come and gone by now.

"See," said Perry. He nudged Nick who studied the billboard with a sardonic smile curling his mouth.

"I think nowadays the slogan is *accelerate your life.*"

"Hoo-boy!" Perry said.

"Hooyah," Nick agreed, amused.

The morning was bitterly cold. The weatherman was prophesying snow for the weekend, although the skies were blue as the belly of an iceberg. Nick and Perry had woken early, fucked lazily and lovingly, and decided to go into the village to see what the sheriff had turned up.

Not that Nick expected a lot of cooperation from the sheriff, but it never hurt to ask — or push. Hard.

A gust of icy wind rattled down the street, blowing the Christmas lights strung through the trees lining the sidewalk, and Perry began to cough.

"Come on, Camille," Nick said. "Let's get you some cocoa."

They went inside the bakery — the same one, Perry pleasantly informed Nick, where Mr. Watson had died — and Nick got a coffee for himself and cocoa and glazed doughnuts for Perry.

"I'll be back in ten minutes; stay here where it's warm," he said briskly, and with that he was gone, vanishing down the street with that quick, purposeful stride.

Perry sat down at one of the little half tables scrunched against the wall beneath a Norman Rockwell calendar and dunked his doughnuts in the cocoa, watching the Christmas shoppers on the street outside

Fifteen minutes passed with no sign of Nick. There was no need to be nervous. It had probably taken him longer than he had expected. If anyone could handle himself, it was Nick. Nor would Nick forget about him and drive back to the estate. Perry's anxiety persisted.

He stepped outside the shop, scanning the busy streets.

"Hey, buddy."

Perry turned. A big man in a blue parka was shoving a paper his way. At first he thought it was a flyer, but then he realized it was a photo.

"You ever see this broad before?"

Perry stared at the man's craggy face. Something about him was familiar, but he couldn't quite place him. He stared at the photograph.

The woman in the picture was young and thin-faced. Her raven hair was styled in one of those big hairdos, her makeup red and harsh.

"Well?" the man demanded. "You seen her around?"

Now Perry remembered him. He was the ugly looking customer from the diner.

Perry concentrated on the woman's bone structure, mentally erasing the eyeliner, the ugly hair... His gaze narrowed. *Holy...!*

It was Jane maybe six or seven years ago. She looked harder, grimmer — and yet there was something haunted and vulnerable in her painted face.

"You do know her," the man said, watching Perry alertly.

Perry looked up, his expression blank. "No." He shrugged. "I don't think so. She looks like a lot of people."

"You know someone else who looks like her?"

Perry shook his head quickly. "I just mean she doesn't seem like anything special."

The man said oddly, "Oh, she's something special, all right." He put the photo back in his jacket pocket.

"Are you a cop?" Perry inquired.

The flat eyes met his own, and Perry felt a little prickle at the back of his neck. "Yeah, that's right. Keep it to yourself, though."

"Sure."

He glanced around, and Nick was striding down the street toward them, his face impassive, but eyes alert. Did he think there was trouble here?

Perry nodded to the man and moved away. The man continued to watch him. Had he done anything to give away his recognition of the photo?

Nick reached him, asking, "Who's your friend?"

Perry glanced back. The man was walking into the bakery.

"I don't think he's anyone's friend."

He told Nick about the photo of Jane back in the day, and Nick said grimly, "He's no cop."

"How do you know?"

Nick shook his head. "I just know. Do you think he believed you about not recognizing the picture?"

"He seemed to." Perry glanced back uneasily. "It doesn't look like he's watching me."

Nick put his hand briefly on Perry's arm. "Yeah, and let's not get caught watching him, or he'll know it's bandits at twelve o'clock."

"If he's not a cop, why would he be asking about Janie?"

"Why don't we ask Jane?" Nick said.

They were in the pickup and on their way back to the estate when Perry remembered to ask, "Did you learn anything at the sheriff's station?"

"They're releasing Teagle. They got confirmation on his alibi. He couldn't have killed Swiss, and even these idiots can see that the two murders are probably connected."

Perry said slowly, "Maybe Miss Dembecki thought Swiss was a burglar and used her trusty poker on him."

"And then what?" Nick questioned. "Shot Tiny when he tried to blackmail her?"

Trying to imagine Tiny having the smarts to attempt blackmail was even harder to picture than Miss Dembecki blowing him away with her trusty .44 Magnum.

Perry shrugged. "Probably not. But I think Janie is right. I think Miss Dembecki is losing it."

"Yeah, I think you're right."

"Did you notice how excited she was at the idea of the passageways?"

Nick nodded.

"And she's been searching the grounds, searching the gazebo." Perry sighed. "She must have been in my rooms for a reason."

Nick kept his eyes on the road. "You think she's looking for the jewels too."

"I do, yeah. If she's getting senile, then I guess there could be another explanation of course, but…"

"That's how I read it," Nick agreed, and Perry felt foolishly flattered.

"What do you think happened? Shane Moran hid the jewels in one of the secret passages and then was killed before he had a chance to retrieve them?"

"Now *that*…I have no idea." Nick considered, chewing. "I guess it's possible. If it's a fact that he and Alston's wife were lovers, she might have told him about the passageways. In fact, he may have already known about them — they may have used those tunnels to smuggle booze into the house. The question is why would Moran stash the jewels at all? Why wouldn't he just leave with them? What would there be to come back for aside from them?"

"Why did he hang around in the woods to get shot?" Perry agreed.

Their eyes met.

"Verity Lane?" Perry suggested.

Nick frowned. "You think he thought she might change her mind about leaving?"

"Maybe."

Nick grimaced. "Then he was pretty stupid."

"Maybe he just really loved her a lot," Perry said quietly.

§ § § § §

There was a local news van parked beside the bridge leading to the Alston Estate. A marked police car blocked its access, but the deputies pulled out of the way for Nick's truck.

Inside the house, Jane was pacing up and down the front hallway.

"Did you see that? There was a news van here a while ago! I called the sheriff on them." She smoothed her hands up and down her upper arms.

"Are you still not feeling well?" Perry asked. Now that he thought about it, he was pretty sure Jane hadn't left the estate in over a week.

She snapped, "This goddamned place is freezing. I think the old bat turned off the furnace."

"Which old bat?" Perry asked.

Jane gave a harsh laugh.

Perry's eyes met Nick's, and he read the message there. "Janie…" he began awkwardly.

As Perry told Jane about the man who was going around town showing her photo, Jane turned paler and paler until she was so white he feared she was going to faint. Nick must have thought so too, because he took her by the arm and guided her to one of the overstuffed chairs by the unlit fireplace.

Jane put her face in her hands. "What did you tell him?" she asked, muffled.

Perry said, "I told him I didn't recognize you."

She looked up, fastening her green gaze on him. "Did he believe you?"

"I don't know."

Nick said, "Even if he did, sooner or later he's going to stumble on someone who knows you from that picture. This is a small town."

Jane nodded. She seemed to be listening to an inner voice. An inner voice delivering some very bad news.

"Who is he?" Perry asked, and Jane's eyes jerked his way.

"I have no idea."

"But…"

She said carefully, "I don't know who he is, but I know who sent him."

"Who?"

Her face worked. At last she said huskily, "Have you ever heard of Michael Cimbelli?"

"No," Perry and Nick said at the same time. Their eyes met.

"Michael is — was — the head of the Martinelli crime family."

Nick said nothing. Perry said, "This is going to be really bad, isn't it?"

Jane said, "I'm not a former hit woman, if that's what you're thinking. I didn't have anything to do with that P.I. getting murdered — or Tiny. This is nothing to do with any of that." She licked colorless lips. "I was Michael's mistress for four years. Then I…left him."

"And he doesn't take rejection well?" Perry asked.

"He doesn't, no. But that wasn't the main problem. I" — she swallowed — "I agreed to testify against Michael in exchange for protection. I went into the Witness Protection Program, but Michael's lawyers were able to delay a trial by claiming that Michael was mentally unfit. They've successfully stalled for three years. Now Michael has been declared competent to stand trial."

"And his goons are looking for you?" Nick finished.

Jane nodded.

"Won't the Witness Protection people move you again?" Perry asked.

"They would," Jane said. "But they don't know where I am, and I don't want them to know."

"*Why?*"

"Because I left the program. I didn't want to live my life like an animal in a cage," she said passionately. "And because of David."

"*David?*"

"Center," Nick supplied.

"I know who she means," Perry said. "I just can't...*David?*"

"Hey," Jane said with a flare of spirit. "You're in no position to talk. You were on the verge of falling in love with a guy on the Internet named *Marcel.* At least I actually *know* David."

Before Perry could respond, Nick said, "Don't they move spouses and lovers into the program?"

Because, Jane's poor choice of men aside, this was the crux of the problem. If Jane went back into the program, she would never see David Center again — which instead of being the relief you'd expect, was apparently tragic enough that she was considering risking her life.

Jane bit her lip and nodded. "They do, but David and I aren't at that point in our relationship. We need more time."

"You don't have more time," Nick said flatly.

Perry and Jane both stared at him.

Nick said, "You can't stay inside this house indefinitely, and even if you could, sooner or later someone in town is going to recognize you from that photo."

"Or," Perry said suddenly, "Your picture is going to turn up on the newswire."

"I have to think," Jane said, rising.

"There's nothing to think about," Nick said. "This is survival time."

Jane did not answer. She went into her apartment and closed the door quietly after her.

"What do we do?" Perry asked Nick.

"Nothing," Nick said. "This is her choice."

"But…"

Nick was already on his way upstairs.

"There's got to be some way we can help her," Perry was saying as they reached Nick's tower room. They could hear the phone ringing from inside.

Nick unlocked the door. "She's a grown-up. She can make her own choices. Stay out of it."

He opened the door and got the phone, and Perry listened to the one-sided conversation while he stared out the window at the bare trees and clouds moving in from the north.

"Just winding things up here," Nick said after the initial greetings were out of the way. That would be Roscoe calling — the former SEAL buddy with the private investigation firm in California.

Perry listened to Nick's silence, and then Nick said slowly, "Another week, but I can probably move it up if I have to."

Perry closed his eyes. When he opened them, he could see the little circle of his breath on the windowpane.

§ § § §

It was a strange day.

Mr. Teagle came home and went straight to his rooms, locking himself in. The sheriff's deputies returned and questioned everyone again, and Perry went over each and every step of coming home from San Francisco and finding the dead man in his bathtub.

"They're trying to work out a timetable," Nick told him. "They've narrowed Swiss's death to Friday afternoon — which lets you and Teagle out, but leaves everyone else here a suspect."

"If Swiss was a private investigator, what was he investigating?"

Nick said, "Apparently, even his secretary didn't know. She'd been on vacation when he took whatever job it was he took on. But here's the thing..." Nick's expression was guarded, as though he knew Perry would not like what he was about to tell him.

"What?"

"Swiss apparently had mob ties."

Perry stared, trying to make sense of this. Then he said indignantly, "No way did Janie kill that guy. And then what? She killed Tiny to keep her secret? No fucking way, Nick!"

"I'm just telling you —"

"Who said he had mob ties?"

"Roscoe." And at Perry's look, Nick explained, "I asked him if he could do a little checking for us."

Us? There was no *us*. Nick wanted this thing wrapped up as fast as possible so he could split for California and not have to give Perry or this place a second thought.

"I don't care what that asshole Roscoe thinks, Jane didn't kill anyone!"

Nick's dark brows rose. "Where the hell is this coming from? Roscoe doesn't think one thing or the other about this. He just ran a name at my request."

"Did you share that information with the sheriff?"

Nick met Perry's glare, unmoved. "No, I didn't. But if you think they won't put this together pretty damn quick, your head is buried as deep in the sand as Bridger's." More patiently, he said, "Come on, Perry. You saw how frightened she was today. If someone came after her, it's possible she might have struck out in a panic. You heard the stuff she said about accidentally killing someone and not being able to come forward."

"She wasn't talking about herself."

"You don't know that."

"What about the Alston sapphires? What happened to that theory? We haven't talked to Mr. Stein."

"I'm sure the cops did, even if they didn't ask him about the sapphires. Besides, what motive would he have for knocking off a Jersey P.I.?"

"According to you, motive doesn't really matter that much. It's all means and opportunity. That was what you said before. And even if she'd known about the secret passage — which I don't believe — Jane wouldn't be able to drag Swiss anywhere. Or Tiny. And the same goes for Miss Dembecki. Which leaves David Center, Mr. Stein, and you."

Nick cut off his immediate exasperated response. He really didn't want to get into an argument with Perry over this. They had little enough time left as it was. He said, "The sheriff is satisfied that Center is not faking his blindness. Which doesn't mean that he couldn't supply the muscle if Bridger needed help carting a body around."

"If they were on those terms, I think Janie wouldn't be worried about his leaving here with her," Perry said tartly.

Nick privately thought he had a point. Which also brought up the fact that if Bridger had killed two people, wouldn't she be calling her pals in Witness Protection to come get her so she wouldn't have to deal with a murder investigation?

He said, "Just because motive isn't the only thing that cops look at doesn't mean it doesn't factor in at all. I never said that."

Perry raised his eyebrows in haughty skepticism — a look that sat oddly on his pointed features. Instead of pissing Nick off, it made him want to laugh, and grab the kid, and wrangle away his bad mood in the best way he knew.

He controlled himself however and said, "I think maybe in this case motive is a factor, and I think the motive of a bunch of loonies searching for some lost sapphires is kind of farfetched."

"You think a million dollars is a farfetched motive?"

"I think those jewels are probably scattered all through the woods. I think I don't want to waste time arguing with you."

That got through. Perry's eyes raised to Nick's, and the set lines of his face relaxed.

"Come here," Nick said softly. "I want to share another one of my theories with you…"

§ § § §

The other event of note that day was Miss Dembecki nearly getting killed when a deputy sheriff, exploring the back passages, opened a wall panel that unexpectedly led onto the grand stairway and nearly knocked her down the steps. Fortunately, Miss Dembecki was nimble enough to escape unscathed.

She scurried back downstairs, locked herself in her rooms, and refused to answer all inquiries through the door as to her health.

"What the hell was she doing climbing up here anyway?" Nick asked.

"I think she was trying to get in my rooms again," Perry said unhappily. "I'm telling you, she thinks the jewels are in this house somewhere."

"I think you're giving her too much credit," Nick said. "I think she's batty."

That seemed to be the consensus of the house. But the only person with a suggestion on what to do about it was Mr. Stein, who voiced the opinion that Mrs. Mac should phone the loony bin posthaste.

By dinnertime the cops had cleared out again, and the rest of the household seemed comfortably locked up behind their doors for the night. Nick made pot roast and commented that he would need to go grocery shopping soon — and then fell awkwardly silent.

Nick would not need to replenish his cupboards. He was going to be leaving very soon and was supposed to be packing even now. Of course, he could always stock up on groceries in the hope that Perry might occasionally remember to eat something.

Perry was not eating much even now, but he was chatting animatedly about an art exhibition he wanted to see in Burlington, and to his astonishment Nick heard himself say, "If I'm still here, I'll go with you."

Perry checked, and then gave Nick one of those dazzling smiles. "It's next month. But yeah, it would have been fun."

Neither of them spoke for a time, and the kitchen was silent but for the scrape of forks on china. Nick said suddenly, roughly, "Why don't you call your parents?"

Perry blinked. "Why?"

"Because you can't —" Nick stopped himself. *What was he doing?* But he couldn't help himself. "Because it's a good time to call. It's almost Christmas. They probably want to hear from you."

They'd have to be pretty fucking cold to shut Perry out of their hearts for good — and Perry was not the product of fucking cold. He'd been sheltered, protected, adored all his life. Mom and Pop Foster were probably sick with worry about him. And lonely. He grew on you, that was for sure.

But Perry said coolly, "They know where to find me. If they wanted to talk to me, they'd get in touch. It's for them to make the first move. I'm not going to apologize for being gay."

You can't make it on your own.

For one horrified second, Nick thought he'd said the traitorous words aloud. It wasn't even true. Perry was surviving. He was relatively healthy, he had a job, a place to stay. He was painting; he was going to make it. It wouldn't be easy, and it would knock a lot of the sweetness and innocence and optimism out of him, but he wasn't a coward.

Nick was the one who was afraid. And what the hell sense did that make? He gritted his jaw against a lot of things he knew he would regret saying, settling for a curt nod and finishing his meal while Perry — not unexpectedly sensitive to his mood — chatted lightly about art and painting and a local artist named Anna Vreman. Anything but murder and sapphires and crazy people.

§ § § §

In wordless accord they turned in early that night, and it was just as good as it had been every time so far — only now it was becoming dangerously, seductively familiar.

And it was safe in the dark to be tender — to be gentle with each other in the dulcet silence. To ask nothing but give everything, caress and kiss, touch and taste until the wanting, longing, needing overswept them again, and they moved in frantic union, breath harsh, the tiny grunts and sighs, the whisper of skin until it rose to a crescendo — the catch in Perry's throat turning to a sob, Nick shouting out once in the keenest of knife-edged pleasure.

"I never really got a chance to see California," Perry said when they were lying quietly, comfortably. "What's it like?"

Nick shrugged. "Warm. Sunny." He almost opened his mouth and made the fatal mistake of saying, "It would be good for you." He caught himself in time, but the thought remained. Instead he said, "Expensive."

Perry nodded. "Do you think you'll ever come back here?"

"To this house?" He was stalling and surprised to find himself doing so. Since when did he pull his punches? He wasn't coming back. Not ever. He couldn't wait to put this place behind him. At least…that had been true until a few days ago. Now…

Now it was harder.

Harder than it should have been.

Perry said dispassionately, "To Vermont, I mean. Some place I could see you again."

He opened his mouth, and Perry said still very calmly, "I mean casually, of course. Just friends. I know how it is."

And that steady acceptance made Nick's chest ache as though he'd fallen wrong on ice. It was hard to get his breath, and he felt cold all the way to his heart.

He said huskily, "I don't know."

A few minutes later he could tell by Perry's breathing that he was asleep. Nick kissed his forehead, and Perry murmured pleasurably. Nick kissed his eyes and his ears and found his mouth, and before long, Perry was awake again, and they were moving against each other.

He yanked down the pajama bottoms with the uncomfortable feeling of robbing the cradle, but Perry wasn't a baby, and he wanted this as much as Nick did — and sooner or later he had to realize that happy endings were for movies. Real life didn't end that tidily. There was a price for everything, and the price for this was that it would be harder for both of them when Nick left — but at the moment, the price seemed worth it.

§ § § §

Perry woke to find himself alone. The sheets were cool where Nick had lain.

This was how it would feel every day after Nick left.

He got up, pulled on jeans, and went into the front room. There was no sign of Nick. No note. He sighed. No use expecting Nick to change.

Deciding to go across the hall to his place and get a change of clothes, he jotted a note for Nick in case he came in while Perry was out.

The house was still. It had a strange, empty feel. He peered over the banister. Not a creature was stirring. Not even Miss Dembecki.

On impulse, he headed downstairs to the basement to grab some boxes. Nick had suggested he start moving his things into Nick's apartment because Nick would be packing for California.

The feeling of being the only person alive in the house persisted. It had never felt like this before. Abandoned.

Wondering if the deputy sheriffs were still parked on the other side of the bridge, he opened the front door. There was no sign of the sheriff's car. No sign of the news van, either.

A gust of wind tasting of approaching snow whipped the lace drapery on the door and sent the chandelier overhead jangling; it sounded like falling icicles. He contemplated the old-fashioned globes and the dangling colored prisms.

An idea slowly dawned.

Looking around, he spotted, still leaning against the staircase, the ladder Tiny had used to fix the leaking windows in the main hall.

He set the ladder up and climbed it. The chandelier was from the 1920s. It was a complicated affair of upturned amber glass shades and individual crystal prisms of blue and gold and red crystal all around an exquisitely painted down-facing glass centerpiece.

Perry studied the centerpiece. Beneath the grime of decades and hand-painted designs of art nouveau flowers appeared to be more colored bits of glass and crystal. His heart began to pound hard with excitement.

It was possible.

Like a lot of the original fixtures in the house, the chandelier no longer worked. Instead of rewiring the old, beautiful lamps and chandeliers, cheap utilitarian lights had been placed at various intervals in the hallways and rooms.

Perry reached up to see if there was a way to dismantle the centerpiece without taking down the whole chandelier. If what he suspected was true, there had to be.

The ladder suddenly jerked out from under him. The thought flashed that he had over-balanced, but as he looked down he saw someone standing beneath him, hands on the ladder.

He grabbed for what support there was — which happened to be the wildly swinging chandelier. It tore out of the ceiling with a horrendous crack of doom.

Then he was falling. The parquet floor rushed up to meet him.

CHAPTER THIRTEEN

The broken chandelier was not a good sign.

Neither was the fact that no one seemed to have noticed it.

Nick hammered on Mrs. Mac's door. There was no sound from inside. No television, no dogs...just an eerie silence.

Down the hallway he could hear sounds of frantic activity. Nick followed the sounds to the kitchen.

"Where is everybody?" he asked.

Miss Dembecki, who was engaged in pulling stuff out of the built-in cupboard drawers of the walk-in kitchen pantry, jumped like a scalded cat.

Like something feral, she stood there facing him down, her gray hair tumbled over the shoulders of her pink bathrobe, her eyes wild. There was a pile of much-yellowed linens around her feet. Embroidered place mats and lace tablecloths, linen napkins. She was clutching a handful of mother-of-pearl napkin rings as though they were her share of a pirate's treasure.

"Where's Perry?" he asked.

She stared at him in that tense but vacant way.

After a pause, Nick said neutrally, "Perry's missing. Mrs. Mac isn't answering her door. Bridger seems to have cleared out."

Miss Dembecki still didn't answer. Nick had the impression that she had not understood him, but then she said, "Miss Bridger has eloped."

"What do you mean she's *eloped*?"

Her eyes flickered at his tone. "She's eloped with Mr. Center. They left during the night." She brightened. "I saw them go. They were carrying suitcases, and they left through the back garden."

"You're sure it was Center she left with?"

Dembecki nodded. "They took Mr. Fluffy too. The men in the black van were waiting for them." She was still watching him with those wide, wary eyes.

"What are you doing?" Nick asked.

To his amazement, she dropped the napkin rings and launched herself at him like a mad thing, hands curved, clawlike, teeth bared. Nick grabbed her wrists and held her away from him as she writhed and snarled.

"Don't think I don't know!" she cried. "I know what you're doing. I know what you're up to. You have his eyes! You can't have mine."

It was like holding onto an animated bundle of rags and bones. Nick held her away from himself while she hissed and screeched at him.

"Lady, I do *not* have time for this," he said crisply. He pushed her back. She fell against the cupboard, glaring at him. Nick picked up the ring of keys lying on the counter, stepped out of the pantry and locked the door behind him. He heard her hit the door a moment later, shrieking.

"Settle down in there," he ordered, but he didn't care if she tore the entire room apart. He couldn't deal with her now. There had been no sign of Perry in his apartment or the tower room or anywhere that Nick could find, and he had a very bad feeling.

He took the stairs fast, went back into his room, and phoned the cops. As he was dialing, he spotted Perry's note about going to the basement for boxes. His guts seemed to crumble away to nothing.

Something had happened to Perry. Something bad.

He could be anywhere in this mausoleum. He could already be dead.

Nick's temples throbbed. He had to take a moment to think.

Okay, odds were good no one was going to try and stash a body — he had to believe a still-live body — in the house. Not with the way the deputies were still prowling through the back.

That left the grounds. The gazebo and the icehouse were his two best bets.

Nick raced down the stairway and cut across the garden. He could hear the rush of the river through the trees, but he refused to consider whether Perry's attacker had simply dumped him into the water.

The gazebo was closer than the icehouse, and he checked it first. He found it empty.

He headed for the icehouse, moving fast and alertly through the wet, frost-etched garden. When he saw the faded building, he became convinced he was right. The icehouse was far enough from the main building to make it ideal for holding someone prisoner.

There would be no point in killing Perry. No need. Just his disappearance was going to have the sheriff combing the place.

No need to kill him. No need to hurt him at all, you fucker.

Frost was melting off the roof of the icehouse in steady, glistening drips. Nick drew his weapon, put his back to the wall, listened.

Silence.

He kicked open the door, ducking back against the wall of the building. The hinges shrieked fit to wake the dead. There was no other sound.

Nick darted a look around the door frame.

It took his eyes an instant to adjust to the lack of light, and then he saw Perry's body at the edge of the pond.

Nick ducked around the doorway. His eyes raked the corners of the cavernous room. All clear.

He holstered his weapon and squelched into the mud, dragging Perry out of the muck onto solid ground. He rolled him onto his back and knelt, wiping the mud from his nose and mouth. He put his face to his and felt very faint puff of breath against his ear.

Nick rocked back on his heels and wiped his arm across his eyes. "Thank you," he muttered.

He ran careful hands over long, motionless limbs, taking stock of the damage. Broken left arm, a knot the size of a goose egg on the side of his head, shocky — but his pulse seemed strong enough.

Perry coughed and opened his eyes. He blinked up at Nick.

"Hooyah," he said.

"Now I know you're concussed." Nick felt over his skull with gentle fingers. "Yep, that's some knock on the head."

"I think I kn-kn...know what happened," Perry told him.

"Yeah?" Nick eased his arm behind Perry's shoulders. "Did it have to do with falling off a ladder?"

"I don't think I fell."

"I think you're right, Humpty Dumpty. I'm going to pick you up. Don't freak."

Perry tensed. "I think my left arm's broken."

"Right again."

"Lucky it's my left."

"Yeah. You are one lucky guy. Hang on, this is going to hurt."

Perry wrapped his good arm around Nick's shoulders, and Nick lifted him. Perry sucked in his breath and swore into Nick's shoulder.

"Hang on."

Perry said conversationally, "Someone yanked the ladder out from under me."

"Did you see who?"

Perry shook his head, sucked in a sharp breath and swore into Nick's neck. "I think I know where the jewels...*ouch!*"

"If they were in the hanging lamp, they're gone now."

Perry didn't answer, breathing hard and fast against Nick's damp skin.

"I'm going to set you down here." Nick followed his words with the action, lowering Perry onto the flat-topped boulder. "I don't want to move you around a lot after a fall like that."

"Yeah, but I don't want to stay here," Perry said, not letting go.

Nick hugged him briefly but carefully. "I've already called the cops. Nothing is going to happen to you in the five minutes it takes me to phone for an ambulance."

"Look at what happened to me the last time you left me alone."

Nick overlooked that. "And then I'll be back with a blanket because you're probably going into shock."

"Great." Perry said as Nick freed himself gently. Perry tried to cradle his broken arm with his other. "Can you make it fast, because I don't feel very good."

"I'm already on my way back," Nick told him, heading for the door. He opened it.

There was a flash of daylight and a loud bang.

Nick staggered back a couple of steps and sat down in the cold water. He sagged slowly back.

"Nick!" Perry yelled. He half jumped, half fell into the pond and hauled Nick into sitting position. He was heavy, and Perry could use only one arm, but he got his head out of the water, got him braced against his knee.

"Jesus," Nick gasped. He tried to push himself to his feet but sank back.

There was blood everywhere, unfurling like smoke through the icy water. Perry's hand felt the obstruction in Nick's back. Nick's pistol.

Instinctively, his hand closed on it, but then froze as a voice said, "Stay where you are. Don't move."

Nick, hand clutched to his shoulder, leaned back against Perry. The shadow blocking the doorway slipped inside the icehouse and pulled the door shut. A flashlight caught them in its beam.

Numb with a lethal combination of pain, shock, and cold, Perry's brain couldn't seem to slip into gear. His thought process was moving so slowly, so inefficiently. Nick was shot. He couldn't take it in. His own arm was killing him.

"He's bleeding," he told the shadow.

"That's the idea."

He recognized the voice without any particular surprise.

"Mr. Stein?"

"You should have stayed out of it, Foster," Stein informed him. "Not that I'm not grateful. I still don't know how the hell you came up with the idea of looking in the chandelier."

Nick tried to turn and see Perry. "You found Moran's stash?"

"I...d-didn't get to see," Perry said through chattering teeth.

Stein said, "Yep, it was in the globe of the chandelier. A fortune in jewels and old coins. It's not everything, but it's a good start. Those people knew how to live." Then he said in a different tone, "You should have taken the hint, Foster. Not dragged your buddy into it."

Perry said stupidly, "The hint?"

"The dead bird," Nick got out between clenched teeth. "That was a warning. A little present from Stein."

"Nope," Stein said, "The dead bird was Tiny's idea. He found it after the storm, and he put it in your room as a warning. Not bad for a retard."

"T-Tiny was in on this?" Now that was truly hard to imagine — Stein partnering up with Tiny. Perry wrapped his hand around the butt of the gun. Nick's body shielded his actions from Stein, but he was never going to be able to use the pistol. Never.

Stein snorted. "Tiny thought he was helping me in undercover work. Hamburger for brains, that one."

"But you heard him talking to Perry and me, and you couldn't trust him not to blab to the real police," Nick said breathlessly. He shifted a little against Perry, and Perry knew he was expecting him to take the pistol. And do what? If he could give it to Nick, it would be one thing…maybe he could drag Nick onto solid ground…

He inched back, and Stein barked, "Don't move, I said!"

"We're freezing."

"Not for long."

Nick grated, "Come on, Stein. How the hell are you going to explain this?"

"I won't have to explain. Who would I have to explain to? Teagle's locked in his room with his porn collection, Mrs. Mac fled to her sister's in Burlington, the Bridger broad and the psychic snuck away last night. The whole mansion is going up in flames tonight, starting with this place. Everyone keeps saying it's a death trap."

"Come off it," Nick said. "The cops aren't as dumb as you think."

"No one knows cops better than me, and these dumb hicks are going to blame the entire thing on that whack job Dembecki."

"Nobody is going to believe Miss Dembecki shot us," Perry said.

"Why not? She's got a gun. She's got Shane Moran's gun. A family heirloom. Bet you didn't know she was Moran's great-grandniece, did you? The old bat's been looking for his loot longer than I have."

"There's no way you can get away with such a crazy —"

"It doesn't matter. I'll be long gone. A new name, a new identity. I know just how to pull it off."

"Somebody's probably called the cops already," Perry said. "A quiet morning like this, shots carry. Miss Dembecki has probably called the cops."

Stein laughed. "You'd better talk to your buddy about that one."

Nick said between clenched teeth, "So why did you kill him? The P.I. Raymond Swiss."

Stein made an aggravated noise. "Would you believe that was an accident," he said. "A total goddamned accident. I bumped into him as I was coming out the secret passage that lets out onto the staircase. He fell down three flights and landed right in front of that moron Tiny." They could hear the shrug in his voice. "That's the kind of luck I have. Or had. Everything's changing now."

"Why did you put him in my tub?" Perry asked. They had to keep Stein talking. He needed time to figure out what to do…

"Tiny said you were gone for the week, so I thought we'd stash him there while I figured things out. I didn't want to take a chance on Teagle stumbling across him while he was prowling through the back passage."

"And then I came back early." *I can't do this,* Perry thought, his hand shaking as he eased the gun from Nick's waistband. *Even if I could hit Stein, which I can't — that little circle of light? I can't shoot someone. I can't…*

If I miss, he'll shoot us both. Now. Immediately. We'll be dead.

Nick asked Stein something else, but Perry's entire concentration was on the weight of the pistol in his shaking hand.

If I could pass the gun to Nick, he thought again.

But if Nick made a move Stein would shoot. He saw — rightly — Nick as the threat.

Nick's breathing sounded weird. Tremors rippled through his body. Shock was probably the least of his problems. He was bleeding to death — freezing to death. And he couldn't do anything but count on Perry to do this, to save them.

Perry felt with his thumb for the safety.

The barrel was wet. Would it even fire?

Nick, game but weakening — still stalling for time — said, "Why didn't you just dump him in the woods after dark?"

And Perry brought the MK23 up and fired at the pinpoint of light. There was a huge explosion, and Perry fell back on his ass. Nick submerged into the water.

There was another bang. Perry kept firing. He could hear Nick splashing around. The rock next to him exploded and flying slivers cut his cheek, his brow.

He tried to get a better line on Stein, slipped in the mud, and his head went under the water. He could see flashes of light as Stein fired back.

And then the gun was yanked out of his hand. A fist fastened in his collar, and he was yanked up, coughing and choking.

"Perry? *Perry!* Are you hit?"

He'd breathed in water so he couldn't talk. Nick was dragging him back behind the jutting teeth of rocks — out of the mud and water. Together they crawled — sloshed behind cover. He could hear someone swearing and crying. It wasn't Nick. It wasn't himself. Stein?

He heaved in breath and let it out as Nick half collapsed on top of him.

"Go for the passage," Nick gasped.

"Not without you."

Nick's voice cracked on something between a sob and a laugh. "What, are you crazy? I'm not staying," he said. "I'm right behind you."

Staying down behind the rocks, they crawled for the passage. Stein fired into the wall, and it was all Perry could do to keep moving.

He felt around for the latch and then found it at last, pressing on what appeared to be one of the beams in the wall. The door swung open and they scuttled through, Perry holding fast to Nick with his good arm. Nick's blood was soaking into his side.

"How bad are you hit?" He gulped. "You should stay still. You're losing blood."

"Move it," Nick panted. "I'll lose more blood if he catches us." He turned and fired a couple of rounds at the entrance behind them.

The stairs were ahead. Perry's breath was catching in his chest, he wheezed desperately helping Nick.

Somehow they made it up the stairs and then staggered down the passage to bobbing lights that were coming toward them swiftly.

It's the light at the end of the tunnel, Perry thought woozily and closed his eyes.

CHAPTER FOURTEEN

Nick hated hospitals, and he had signed the Against Medical Advice form practically as soon as he could sit up. He was not in any shape to pack and leave for California, of course, and in any case there were a number of things he had to take care of first — not the least of which was signing for the cops his statement regarding the recent violent events at the Alston Estate.

Perry did not enjoy hospitals, but since — in addition to his broken arm, cracked ribs, and concussion — he had developed a mild case of pneumonia, he was relieved to find himself in a hospital surrounded by lots of starchy personnel. He felt safe there.

When Nick came to see him — interestingly pale for Nick and with his arm in a sling, but still somehow looking alive and vital and very tough — Perry managed a two-finger salute and a flicker of a smile. He fell almost immediately back to sleep — not sure if Nick really did sit down next to his bed or if he dreamed it.

There was nothing to be afraid of any more. He was alive. Nick was alive. Nothing else seemed very important.

The police came and took his statement and then went away again.

Perry began to feel better. He began to worry about the fact that he was in the hospital without health insurance and that his vacation was now over, and that Nick would be leaving soon. Maybe Nick was already gone?

But then Nick came to see him again.

"How are you doing?" he asked briskly. He smelled like the wintery outdoors and like his herbal soap — a nice change from the antiseptic smells of the hospital.

"Good," Perry said, although he looked wan and uncomfortably elfin in Nick's opinion.

Perry nodded to the enormous fruit basket on the cabinet by the bed. "Have an apple."

Nick examined the basket. There was no return address, but the card said, *Wish me luck. And I'll wish you the same. Janie.*

That reminded him, and he brought Perry up to speed on what was happening at the Alston Estate. Poor Miss Dembecki had been sent to a state mental hospital, Jane and David Center had disappeared back into the Witness Protection Program, and Mrs. Mac was advertising for new tenants.

Perry asked carefully, "Is Stein... I didn't kill him or anything?"

"Nah, he'll be arraigned as soon as he gets out of the hospital." Nick grinned briefly. "You shot him twice, and you managed not to hit a vital area. You're either one hell of a marksman or the worst shot in the world."

"It's hard when they shoot back," Perry said.

"Yeah."

"Was Miss Dembecki really Shane Moran's niece?"

"Yeah. Apparently she grew up on legends of her infamous great-great-uncle. The story is a couple of Moran's gang got away, and after Moran was killed, they went to his sister and told her that Verity Lane was in on the whole heist. Moran left the jewels with her, she hid them — nobody but she knew where apparently — and then the plan was she was going to run away with Moran. But he was killed and she had some kind of breakdown and that was apparently that. She left her husband and moved to France and apparently never thought of the jewels again.

"Wow. How did Mr. Stein get involved?"

"He's not talking."

Nick was already prowling restlessly around the room, clearly impatient to be on his way. Perry asked, striving to keep his voice neutral, "When are you leaving?"

"A couple of days. Right after Christmas."

Perry nodded.

"I'll have to come back for the trial," Nick told him, and Perry smiled.

"That's true."

Nick took another turn around Perry's half of the bare little room and then said, "I called your folks."

"You…"

Nick avoided Perry's gaze. "I got the number from Mrs. Mac, and I called them. They had a right to know."

He glanced at Perry, and Perry was so still he didn't appear to be breathing. Nick said, "They want to see you, but they'll respect your wishes if you don't want to see them."

"Why wouldn't I want to see them?" Perry said faintly.

"I think they feel pretty bad about some of the things they said. Anyway, they're staying here in the village if you feel like calling them." Nick laid a slip of paper on Perry's tray.

"Yeah, I want to see them," Perry said, and his eyes got very bright and his voice got husky. He cleared it. "Are you —"

And at the same time Nick said, "I should be going."

"Oh, right." Perry looked very tired. He smiled at Nick and said, "Will I…will you stop in to say good-bye?"

"That's pretty much what this is," Nick said firmly.

Perry looked more tired than ever, but he still managed something like a smile. "Right. Well, thanks. I mean, thanks isn't much…"

Nick covered his mouth with a quick hard kiss. Perry kissed him back hard and resisted the urge to wrap his arms around Nick and say a lot of things that would guarantee Nick didn't look him up when he came back for the trial.

"Take care of yourself, kid," Nick said gruffly, and he was gone — out the door and down the corridor before Perry opened his eyes.

§ § § §

Perry's parents had been almost exactly as Nick had pictured. Pop was ex-marine and owned his own contracting business. Mom was of the stay-at-home school, everything in apple-pie order and neat as a pin. Very nice people. Good people. People of limited imaginations but the best intentions — and they loved Perry every bit as much as Nick had figured they did. Perry came by his stubbornness honestly, but the horror of learning what had nearly befallen their frail little darling in the big bad world had made them desperate to get him comfortably back in the nest, where hopefully he would outgrow his unhealthy attachment to other boys, but either way, he'd be safe beneath the parental wing.

Nick knew he had done the right thing by contacting them. No way did he want the kid left on his own for Christmas, and as for himself…well, a clean break was the best thing for both of them. He was ten years older and a lifetime harder than Perry, and frankly he didn't want to queer the deal — literally — in Los Angeles by showing up with his gay lover. He didn't know how far Roscoe's tolerance stretched — he didn't know anything about the partners — and he couldn't afford to blow this chance.

Maybe if Perry had…kicked a little, tried to talk him out of it, showed a little backbone…because the kid did have guts and he was stubborn, and if he wasn't fighting, then maybe he knew Nick was right.

Nick knew he was right. He was just surprised at how hard it was. But that was mostly the season. It was easy to feel lonely around the holidays, and he actually preferred being lonely on his own to being lonely with Marie.

All the same, if he heard "I'll Be Home for Christmas" one more time, he was going to shoot someone.

He was packing the last few odds and ends on Christmas Eve when someone knocked on his door.

He opened the door, and Perry stood there. He was wearing a new leather jacket over his shoulders — beneath the jacket, his arm was in a cast. He looked very thin and too pale — and there was something about his expression…

He looked older.

"Merry Christmas," he said, and awkwardly, one-handed Nick a square box.

Nick took the box without glancing at it. "What are you doing here? Are you supposed to be out of the hospital? Your folks came to see you, right?" Sudden anxiety gripped him at the thought of Perry let down yet again.

Perry nodded. "Yeah. Can I come in?"

Nick fell back automatically, and Perry came inside saying, "They've been here all week. They came to see me every day — unlike you."

Nick had bent to set the wrapped package on the floor, but at that he straightened. "We said good-bye," he said. There was absolutely no reason to feel guilty, but somehow the words got away from him. "Anyway, I thought you'd be on your way home."

"This *is* my home," Perry said. "Or did you change your mind about letting me stay here after you leave?"

And now Nick's anxiety bloomed into genuine worry. "Why would you need to stay here? Everything's fine with your folks, isn't it?"

"Sure."

Nick couldn't quite read him. "So…where are they?"

"On their way back to Rutland."

"Why aren't you with them?"

Perry stared at him. "Why would I be? I'm an adult and I have my own life. You know, the one you don't want any part of."

Color flooded Nick's face. "Hey…"

Perry's control slipped for a moment, and he said bitterly, "I'm not a puppy, Nick. You don't need to give me away to a good home when you move away."

"Now look," Nick said warningly. He wasn't angry, though, despite the hard pounding of his heart and the flush suffusing his body. All that adrenaline and no place to go…

"It's okay," Perry said. "You've been very clear about it from the start. It's my own fault if I kept hoping that maybe you cared a little more than you said you did."

"I never said I didn't care."

"You never said anything at all."

"Neither did you."

"I love you," Perry said. "But you already know that. Except you don't think I'm old enough to know what love is."

Nick snapped, "I never said that."

"Like I said, you never said *anything*."

"Okay, well for the record, I do care. I…care. But…" Nick swallowed hard.

"But what?" Perry asked. "Oh yeah. You're going to California and it's expensive."

"*That* doesn't have anything to do with it!"

Perry didn't say anything, and newly awkward with him, Nick said, "Well, it's your place now. Sit down."

But Perry didn't sit. He went to the window and stared out. Nick looked from his stiff back and squared shoulders to the brightly wrapped Christmas present and said, "Should I open this now?"

"If you want. It's not really your kind of thing," Perry said. "It's a snow globe. You know, a big old house and lots of Vermont snow. I thought it might remind you of me."

"I don't need a snow globe to remind me of you," Nick said, which was probably the most romantic thing he had ever heard himself say. It made him blush.

Perry seemed unimpressed, though. He turned away from the window to face Nick. "So when are you leaving?"

Nick hesitated. Was he still going? Suddenly he wasn't so sure. He said, "Tomorrow morning. I'm staying overnight in town."

"I'll drive you."

"With a broken arm?"

"Okay, you drive me."

"I sold my truck," Nick said. "Teagle is going to drive me."

Perry nodded thoughtfully. "How about this? We can spend tonight together, and you can get a taxi in the morning."

And Nick suddenly recognized what that unfamiliar emotion was rushing through him — the warmth and excitement and anticipation. *Happiness.*

He said, "How about this? Why don't I call and postpone my flight. Is it going to take you more than a week to pack?" He fastened his hand on Perry's shoulder and drew him forward.

Perry's mouth quirked. He seemed to consider it, eyelashes downcast. Then he looked up, and the expression in his eyes made Nick's breath catch. "What happens if it does?"

Against his will, Nick's mouth was curving into a smile. He had the uncomfortable feeling that was going to be happening a lot. He said, "I wait another week."

Perry smiled that slow, engaging grin. "Okay."

Their lips met, slow and sweet — they were getting better at this part too — and Christmas and homecoming coalesced into something unexpectedly hot and hungry.

When they broke for air at last, Nick said, "Goddamn it, Foster. I had this all worked out."

"Yeah, sorry." Perry leaned back in, and his mouth smiled against Nick's.

"What?" Nick asked suspiciously.

Perry said, "Oh, you know. Let the journey begin."

About the Author

JOSH LANYON is the author of numerous novellas and short stories as well as the critically praised Adrien English mystery series. THE HELL YOU SAY was shortlisted for a Lambda Literary Award and is the winner of the 2006 USABookNews awards for GLBT fiction. In 2008, Josh released MAN, OH MAN: WRITING M/M FICTION FOR KINKS AND CA$H, the definitive guide to writing for the m/m or gay romance market. Josh lives in Los Angeles, California, and is currently at work on the fifth book in the Adrien English series. You can visit Josh at his website: www.joshlanyon.com.

THE TREVOR PROJECT

The Trevor Project operates the only nationwide, around-the-clock crisis and suicide prevention helpline for lesbian, gay, bisexual, transgender and questioning youth. Every day, The Trevor Project saves lives though its free and confidential helpline, its website and its educational services. If you or a friend are feeling lost or alone call The Trevor Helpline. If you or a friend are feeling lost, alone, confused or in crisis, please call The Trevor Helpline. You'll be able to speak confidentially with a trained counselor 24/7.

The Trevor Helpline: 866-488-7386

On the Web: http://www.thetrevorproject.org/

THE GAY MEN'S DOMESTIC VIOLENCE PROJECT

Founded in 1994, The Gay Men's Domestic Violence Project is a grassroots, non-profit organization founded by a gay male survivor of domestic violence and developed through the strength, contributions and participation of the community. The Gay Men's Domestic Violence Project supports victims and survivors through education, advocacy and direct services. Understanding that the serious public health issue of domestic violence is not gender specific, we serve men in relationships with men, regardless of how they identify, and stand ready to assist them in navigating through abusive relationships.

GMDVP Helpline: 800.832.1901

On the Web: http://gmdvp.org/

THE GAY & LESBIAN ALLIANCE AGAINST DEFAMATION/GLAAD EN ESPAÑOL

The Gay & Lesbian Alliance Against Defamation (GLAAD) is dedicated to promoting and ensuring fair, accurate and inclusive representation of people and events in the media as a means of eliminating homophobia and discrimination based on gender identity and sexual orientation.

On the Web: http://www.glaad.org/

GLAAD en español:

http://www.glaad.org/espanol/bienvenido.php

SERVICEMEMBERS LEGAL DEFENSE NETWORK

Servicemembers Legal Defense Network is a nonpartisan, nonprofit, legal services, watchdog and policy organization dedicated to ending discrimination against and harassment of military personnel affected by "Don't Ask, Don't Tell" (DADT).The SLDN provides free, confidential legal services to all those impacted by DADT and related discrimination. Since 1993, its inhouse legal team has responded to more than 9,000 requests for assistance. In Congress, it leads the fight to repeal DADT and replace it with a law that ensures equal treatment for every servicemember, regardless of sexual orientation. In the courts, it works to challenge the constitutionality of DADT.

SLDN
PO Box 65301
Washington DC 20035-5301
On the Web: http://sldn.org/

Call: (202) 328-3244
or (202) 328-FAIR
e-mail: sldn@sldn.org

THE GLBT NATIONAL HELP CENTER

The GLBT National Help Center is a nonprofit, tax-exempt organization that is dedicated to meeting the needs of the gay, lesbian, bisexual and transgender community and those questioning their sexual orientation and gender identity. It is an outgrowth of the Gay & Lesbian National Hotline, which began in 1996 and now is a primary program of The GLBT National Help Center. It offers several different programs including two national hotlines that help members of the GLBT community talk about the important issues that they are facing in their lives. It helps end the isolation that many people feel, by providing a safe environment on the phone or via the internet to discuss issues that people can't talk about anywhere else. The GLBT National Help Center also helps other organizations build the infrastructure they need to provide strong support to our community at the local level.

National Hotline: 1-888-THE-GLNH (1-888-843-4564)
National Youth Talkline 1-800-246-PRIDE (1-800-246-7743)
On the Web: http://www.glnh.org/
e-mail: info@glbtnationalhelpcenter.org